Home on Star Island

Home on

HOUGHTON MIFFLIN COMPANY · BOSTON
New York · Atlanta · Geneva, Ill. · Dallas · Palo Alto

Star Island

by Christina M. Welch

Illustrated by Robert MacLean

Merit Book Edition 1970
HOUGHTON MIFFLIN COMPANY

PUBLISHED BY ARRANGEMENT WITH LITTLE, BROWN & COMPANY

COPYRIGHT © 1962 BY CHRISTINA MARQUAND WELCH

LIBRARY OF CONGRESS CATALOG CARD NO. 62-12385

PRINTED IN THE UNITED STATES OF AMERICA

To my children
C. H. W.
R. E. W. III
C. S. W.
E. M. W.
M. C. W.

Contents

Home on Star Island

A Short Voyage

THE SUN was setting on a day in early May when a fishing sloop neared the Isles of Shoals. The ocean reflected the sky's pink and its currents were a deep purple. A quiet easterly wind filled the sloop's large sail. Small waves softly slapped against the boat's sides.

A gentle evening, Isaac Mason thought, as he steered his sloop to one of the larger rock islands. He gazed up at some sea gulls circling above the mast. They were calling to one another in a hungry manner.

One settled on the topsail to scold Mr. Mason. The bird puffed his gray chest out, batted his great wings up and down, and called out fussily to Mr. Mason again and again. His yellow eyes shot tiny sparks of fury.

"None of that now. No fish for you this evening,"

Mr. Mason shouted to him. The gull continued scolding like a petulant old man.

Isaac Mason had known this bird for three long years, and had affectionately named him Siras. During the late spring and summer months Siras knew just when Isaac would row his dory out to the sloop anchored in the small harbor off Star Island. An hour before sunrise, when a pearl-white mist was melting the night's darkness away, Siras would be seen perched in the stern of the dory with two fishermen, members of Isaac's crew. His yellow eyes snapped at Isaac through the dim light as if to say, "Are the waves going to get the better of your oars and sails today?"

Arriving at the sloop, Siras would fly up to the top rigging to supervise the fishermen unfurling the sails. Strutting up and down, he would order one sail to be made taut, and warn the sailors to keep a sharp eye out for a sudden west wind. The sight of a sagging jib would throw him into a screaming rage.

At last, impatient at being bossed about, Isaac Mason would shout, "Who is captain of this ship, you or I?" Often he would ask himself which of the two really was.

When the sloop was finally in order, it would sail out to the trawls placed sometimes as much as twenty miles off the Isles of Shoals. Once there, Isaac would give Siras the first small fish he pulled in from the cold Atlantic, be it a cod or a mackerel. Siras was not particular about his breakfast and would fly happily back to the Shoals with the fish clamped tightly in his beak. There he would wait for Isaac's safe return from a trip to Portsmouth with his catch. No matter what luck befell Isaac Mason, whether the day was stormy or the catch poor, he always remembered to save an especially tender herring for Siras's supper.

On this particular evening Siras had good reason to be outraged. All day he had looked forward to his delicious supper only to discover that Isaac Mason had let him down. He simply could not believe that there was no supper. Nothing was left for him to do but scold and flap his wings at Isaac, the crew, the heavens, and the waves.

"Stop that fussing up there," Isaac yelled gruffly. "Go fish for your own supper."

To himself Isaac softly remarked, "I am sorry. But I have a strange cargo to deal with today."

Being a rather solitary man who knew mostly about fish and sailors, Isaac had found this cargo a worrisome thing. It had taken his mind off his sailing, which should never happen to a man even in fair weather. Yet he rather liked this different catch. He glanced about the boat in order to check on it. Fortunately it was still there in fairly good order.

A boy named Caleb stood near the bow seriously studying the rock islands ahead of him. Close beside him was his pigtailed sister, Rebecca, whose brown eyes gazed wistfully at the great ocean.

Now and then Rebecca inspected the treasures in her little knapsack: a wooden doll, a ball of yarn and knitting needles, three picture books and two photographs. She felt of each one of them, as though the objects kept sad thoughts from her mind.

At times she cast an anxious look at Sarah, her plump little sister, who had been trotting gaily about the boat. Sarah had been so busy calling to the waves and gulls that she finally had become quite weary. Now she sat quietly in the bow. She stared solemnly at Siras in the rigging and at the clear sky above him, while the rays of the setting sun touched her light hair, turning it to the purest gold.

"Sunset is a pensive time. Especially for these quiet ones who have just learned about real sadness," Isaac murmured.

He had known the children's father only slightly, but their grandparents, old Mr. and Mrs. Deane, had spent their lives in Gosport village on Star Island. Mr. Deane was as silent and weather-beaten as the rocks

about him. It was hard to think of him as having anything to do with children, but long ago he had had a son, Samuel. About the time Samuel was born, Mr. Deane suddenly had given up all his fishing and whaling. It was as though the son had brought a fearful hatred of the sea to him.

Never allowed to go out fishing with his friends, the boy had led a rather lonely life on Star Island. Old Mr. Deane put Samuel to work in his village store counting change and merchandise and attending to the customers. When Samuel grew up the little store couldn't hold him. He went away to Salem and soon opened up one of the finest shops in that town. A few Gosport villagers who had visited it returned saying that it was full of rare merchandise, silks, jade, Canton china, and delicious candied ginger.

Samuel paid several visits to his parents, but after a while word got around the village that he had a bride. She was a Miss Whipple, a member of an old seafaring family. Her father and grandfather were both captains of their own vessels, and her brothers were fishermen or West Indian traders.

The Gosport villagers claimed that old Mr. Deane was fearful that a member of this family would eventually lead his son out to sea and to his death. The fear nagged at Mr. Deane for years, and because of it, and because Salem seemed so very far away to him, almost at the end of the earth, neither he nor Mrs. Deane ever saw their son or his young wife after the marriage.

Isaac sometimes felt that it was Mr. Deane's strong fear which mysteriously made the dreaded event come true. It had happened the previous October. Samuel Deane's brother-in-law and some of his fishermen friends persuaded Samuel to go out with them on a two-day fishing trip. There were squalls at sea, and on the first night out Samuel Deane was swept overboard.

When old Mr. Deane heard the news he simply gave up speaking. Day after day he strode to the store, his head bent, scowling at the rocks and earth. If it hadn't been for his kindly helper, Jim Peacham, the villagers would not have dared to enter his shop. To them he became the fiercest and saddest sight on Star Island.

Samuel Deane left his wife with the large store and three growing children to care for. Heartache, her new responsibilities, and the long, damp winter finally brought on illness and she took to her bed.

" 'Twas just three weeks back that she died," Isaac said to himself. He gazed out at the peaceful sea, wondering at the wickedness lying beneath its calm surface. "But there's the living to consider," he thought.

That afternoon the Salem stagecoach had left the three children standing on the Portsmouth pier. It had been Isaac's task to meet them and sail them out to the Isles of Shoals, where they were to live with their grandparents.

He thought of their solemn, pale faces. Shaking his head doubtfully he said, half aloud, "I do hope they will like their new home. 'Twill take some time and some doing."

Suddenly a harsh squawk pierced the air. Siras, the old gull, was vigorously scolding Sarah in her corner. The child had upset a bucket of bait and was trying to clutch all the slippery minnows at once. Her calico skirt was drenched in brine and Siras was pecking at her red cape.

"Here, she's no match for the likes of you," Isaac shouted as he hurried over to the pair.

He took some minnows which Sarah was not quite sitting on and gave them to the gull. "Here's your supper, old man."

Sarah screeched and looked angrily up into Isaac's face. Isaac looked into hers. After a terrible instant, she switched into pure laughter. He looked hard into the little giggling face, not believing what he had seen there at first. Maybe he had been mistaken, but he was certain that she had stuck out her tongue at him.

"You try doing that to your old grandfather," he said with a laugh.

At the Landing

THE EARLY evening breezes gently blew the fishing sloop into the little harbor of Star Island. On reaching his destination, Isaac Mason swiftly tied his boat to the mooring and then went to work letting down and tying up the sails.

Caleb and Rebecca watched his steady motions knowing that there was no need for him to pause and inspect his surroundings, because this harbor was a part of his home. They looked at the low rock islands that protected the harbor on three sides from the Atlantic Ocean. The rocks sheltered a group of rough gray dories, some weather-beaten fishing sloops, and several larger and more freshly painted schooners. At this hour they were all safely rocking at their moorings.

Isaac Mason helped Caleb haul the children's luggage to the leeward side of his sloop. He then slid into his dory, which was fastened to the same mooring, and brought it around to the boat's side. With Caleb's help the luggage and Rebecca were safely installed in the dory.

Sarah scampered over to her particular corner of the sloop to snatch a handful of minnows from Isaac's bait bucket.

"Put those back," Caleb ordered in a frightened tone.

She stood still, and firmly shook her head.

"Leave those there. Your grandma wants you home by suppertime and without any dead minnows," Isaac called.

At the sound of this stranger's voice she dropped her fish and trotted obediently to Caleb. Caleb lowered her into the dory and then slid in beside her. The three children sat together on the long seat in the stern while Isaac rowed steadily towards the Star Island pier. He glanced at the set faces of Caleb and Rebecca. Their mouths were like sharp little pencil lines and their solemn eyes were riveted to Star Island and its landing.

The children saw a pathway sloping down the rocky hill from Gosport village to the small, pebbly beach and pier. Some boats were laid up on the shore waiting to be recalked and painted for the summer. There were two groups of fishermen mending various nets and lobster pots.

Several women, some carrying large baskets filled with driftwood or clams, stood in a circle just above the pier. Their heads were together as they busily talked. Now and again one of them pointed to Isaac's dory.

"We're here," Rebecca exclaimed so loudly that she surprised herself.

Isaac's dory slipped alongside the pier while he drew his oars in. Another fisherman came to help him fasten the dory and start the business of unloading the little boat.

Caleb and Rebecca were the first of the cargo to be hoisted up to the pier. They stood stiffly frozen to the end of it.

Some barefoot boys played tag on the beach. One redheaded lad shouted, "Hey, Isaac, did you catch me a sea horse today?"

Rebecca's eyes traveled to a spot beyond the carefree boys. Clutching Caleb's arm, she whispered excitedly, "Is that our grandmother?"

Above the pier, seated on a rock by herself, was the oldest woman they had ever seen. She was dressed in black wool. Her hair trailed down her shoulders in mats and spikes of steel gray. Great crevices cut paths about her yellowed face and pointed chin. A corncob pipe stuck firmly in her thin mouth. She rocked back and forth cackling to herself and appeared to stare into the sunset.

Suddenly she sat up straight and pointed a long finger at the dory. A sharpness in her cackling voice carried her words to the children. "Did you bring the wee ones with you, Isaac? We want to see the wee ones."

"Oh no," murmured Caleb. "She couldn't be our grandmother."

Despite his words, Caleb lowered his eyes and grasped Rebecca's hand, dreading that the old hag might come down to claim them. After a while he dared to look up at the old woman again. She rocked back and forth, still cackling to herself. Suddenly her black eyes became still as she gazed down at the dory. A peal of harsh laughter reeled through her long frame.

The children heard a splash beside the dory. A red cape bobbed along on top of a mild ocean swell.

"Sarah!" Caleb and Rebecca cried in one voice.

Instantly Isaac's friend, the fisherman, was in the water handing the wet bundle up to Isaac. For a minute Isaac sat in the dory with the little girl in his arms. Sarah was quiet, feeling the cold wetness chilling her entire body. She stared blankly at the gentle waves.

"If anything had ever happened to Sarah," Rebecca half sobbed to Caleb.

She saw Sarah toddling out of bed in the early morning, her whole face smiling, beckoning her brother and sister on to the surprises of a new day. She saw Sarah walking down a Salem street, as grown-up as you please, with her bonnet turned backwards. In her father's sunny yard, Sarah had affectionately sung to her dolls only suddenly to spank them all soundly and hide them under a bush.

"She is so naughty," Rebecca stated mournfully, "but where would the fun be without her?"

With silent thankfulness Caleb and Rebecca watched Isaac hoist Sarah up on the dock. Kneeling down beside the little girl, they tried to keep her warm by putting their arms about her. Cold water ran down Sarah's skirts and petticoat, and she watched it helplessly through her quiet tears as it formed tiny pools and streams on the dock. Rebecca stroked her chilled golden hair.

"Here's a blanket," said a gruff voice.

Standing before the children was a large, solid man

with a thick gray beard and heavy white eyebrows. He stared at Sarah as though she were some strange piece of driftwood which he had never seen before.

Tossing down on the dock a black blanket, which smelled strongly of fish, he placed Sarah in the middle of it and speedily wrapped her up. He flung her over his shoulder. With giant steps he strode away, carrying his enormous satchel.

The children started after him, but before they had a chance to catch up to him, they were stopped by the sight of a stout, rather fluttery woman who half ran along the dock. She called out, addressing no one in particular, "How did it happen? How terrible! A near escape. Poor lamb."

When she reached Caleb and Rebecca, she threw up her hands to the skies. A smile circled about the whole lower half of her face and broke up the rest of it into many ripples.

The children were struck by how rosy her plump cheeks were. "Like those painted on my wooden doll," Rebecca thought.

"My little children, all safe and sound," the woman cried. "Thank you, Isaac Mason," she called down to the dory. "Thank you for bringing my little pigeons. Could you follow us with their baggage, as we must make haste?"

She paused and drew in a deep breath of sea air. Her eyes turned to the children." Come along, my duckies," she sang in her high-pitched voice and began to trot down the dock, her vast skirts jerking from side to side.

Rebecca glanced down at Isaac, trying to discover whether they should go with her or not.

Isaac nodded. "Yes, get along with you. That's your grandmother."

He watched them running a little cautiously behind their grandmother. They passed the ancient woman seated on her rock. Isaac heard her cackle, "Ah, here are the wee ones. Safe and snatched from the sea, snatched from the sea."

The children stopped to glance at her and then hurriedly stumbled on their way up the path.

"If anyone can, Mrs. Deane will shatter the sadness of those children into a million pieces," Isaac remarked to the darkening evening.

The Scarlet Pimpernel

"Oh dear, I have been running a trifle more than my age allows," gasped Mrs. Deane as she halted beside the door of a medium-sized stone cottage.

A small flower garden lay snugly beside the house. It had many late-blooming daffodils. Some morning-glories ran through them and were on the verge of climbing up the cottage wall. Wide mustard bushes sheltered the garden on either end and lined the other sides of the cottage.

Mrs. Deane threw open the low gray door. "Here we are," she said, and pushed Caleb and Rebecca over the threshold.

The children found themselves in a fairly large, low-ceilinged room. Tall windows were on either side, with deep window seats built into them.

"They would be nice to curl up in with a book," Rebecca thought.

Towards one end of the room was a long table already set for supper. In a dim corner beyond it Rebecca saw a pine cupboard. Opposite stood a spinning wheel.

There was a large fireplace at the other end of the room. The children's grandfather loomed before it, his huge boots and long legs partially concealing a blazing fire. He scowled hard at the floor where Sarah sat, sockless, on the black blanket.

Rebecca, disregarding the large figure, hastened towards the little girl.

"No time for dawdling," chimed Mrs. Deane in her high voice. "There are hungry children to be fed. Thomas, you light the lamps so we can see a thing or two in here. Caleb and I will get dinner on the table."

A hum of pleasant bustle came over the room while Rebecca briskly undressed Sarah and dried her by the fire. She took out Sarah's favorite red-checked blouse from one of the packing cases.

"The blouse might make you feel warm and important in this new place," Rebecca whispered.

Sarah did not answer. She stood limply in front of Rebecca, allowing her sister to do what she wished to with her. Her lips were blue from her recent chill and her pale face was tense. Her blue eyes were wide with bewilderment as she inspected the new surroundings.

"Dinner is ready," Mrs. Deane called.

The two girls advanced slowly towards the table and quietly sat down with the rest of the family.

Caleb spied a piece of hot corn bread resting temptingly at the side of his plate. Quickly he devoured it, unaware that all eyes were momentarily fixed upon him. He put his right hand down to continue his dinner with a fork when, much to his surprise, his knuckles received a sharp rap from a pewter knife.

The Grandfather, who sat beside him, frowned darkly down on him. The thick white eyebrows were so knotted that they could not possibly come undone.

Unshed tears stung Caleb's eyes.

The Grandmother smiled wistfully at him over her steaming bowl. Then she bowed her head.

"Bless this food and us to thy service. Amen."

Why couldn't he have remembered? At home they had all said grace before every meal. But nothing was very real way out here in the middle of the ocean.

Caleb recalled the real things, the noise from the Salem streets, their kitchen with its cheery, potbellied stove, his father singing sea chanteys off key. His mother had always made corn bread for him on special occasions like Christmas and birthdays.

Out here all was so different. This was not even a birthday. He was surrounded by shadows. There was a large, fierce one on his right. Even the lively Sarah was but a whisper of herself as she stared fixedly at her plate.

Wherever had his parents gone? As long as he wasn't with them, he felt that they must be caring for other children and tucking them into bed. He could not think of his mother and father without children.

"It will be hard for you to get used to our island ways. But in time you will be scrambling about like wild goats." The Grandmother chatted quietly on, while the children slowly ate their dinner.

Dinner was concluded by a heavy silence.

The Grandfather pushed his chair from the table. Only a trace of his scowl remained. He looked straight ahead, beyond his wife, out of the window at some distant point in the night. His voice was deep, but surprisingly mild. The words came slowly, as though each had a little existence of its own.

"This evening puts me in mind of Solomon White, an old sea captain. His ship was wrecked on Duck Island, not far from here, one November night. All hands were drowned, the fine ship was in splinters, and the cargo, which he had carefully collected and which was to bring him his fortune, was buried under the waves.

"An old hag who was out searching for fagots spied him lying on the rocks the next morning. She rowed him over here to Star and the doctor, seeing that one of his legs was gone, pegged a wooden one on. He also found Solomon a little hovel down at the end of the street. There old Solomon lived for one winter. The inside of his house was black with coal smoke. The place reeked of rum and old pork. His gray hair was down to his shoulders. His skin was as black and greasy as a whale's back. He was a sight folks feared to look at.

"No one ever knew what Solomon thought about all that long winter, but I could guess. All was lost. He had been living with ships and the sea ever since he was a lad. The day came when he had earned the command of his own vessel. This was his prize and in one storm it was wiped away. 'Twas no use living after that.

"Well, he went on drinking and wanting to throw himself into the sea when he heard a light knocking at his door one spring morning. He opened it and there was a little girl who thrust a bunch of scarlet pimpernel and a sack of fresh eggs into his grimy hands. She skipped away before he could blink his bloodshot eyes."

"How did she dare do that?" inquired Rebecca, quite forgetting her timidity.

The Grandfather's eyes rested intently upon her.

"Oh, there are some children who have the daring of the wildest of birds," he responded. "A very queer thing happened after that. The eggs and pimpernel must have seemed so sweet and fresh to him after being shut up in that dismal shack that he wanted to see what else was new in the world. He walked over the whole island. The southern breezes worked into his clogged lungs. He saw the gulls collecting odd shells and twigs for their nests. He watched the children doing their chores. Later on he must have seen the fishermen coming in with their catch. Straightways he knew that he must again sort of join the world. He fell to building dories. The sturdiest dories this isle has yet to see. People used to sail out from the coast just to see them, and even now some fishermen boast of owning one of Solomon White's dories.

"Something else happened. He turned to cleaning up his shack and being a kind gentleman who was looked up to by all of us. Most likely he was that sort of man until the trouble struck him. There's no doubt that his old self was blown back to him on that spring morning. It was all because of the little girl who gave him the scarlet pimpernel and fresh eggs."

The Grandfather looked hard at the listening faces around his table. He did not smile but a satisfied look settled on his face. "I'm no good at it, but perhaps, in her way, your grandmother can hand you young ones some fresh eggs and scarlet pimpernel, as she did, many years ago, to a sad, lonely old man."

"Were you that little girl?" Rebecca asked her grandmother in a hushed voice.

The Grandmother nodded. She blushed a little as she met the wide eyes of all three of her grandchildren.

"It's hard to think of me as I was then," she apologized. "I had Rebecca's long brown pigtails."

The children pictured that clear, fresh morning. The shy girl's hand trembled as she gave her gifts to the grimy old man and then ran away over the rocks.

Mrs. Deane shattered their thoughts briskly.

"Now it's time for bed. Up with all three of you."

Carrying a lamp, she led the way up a narrow flight of stairs to their little rooms.

"These are tiny but they need children all the same," she explained as she showed Caleb a small room with a sloping ceiling. A cot stood near a dormer window and there was a washstand in one corner with a white china pitcher and bowl on top.

She took the girls into the next room, which was exactly the same except for a large double bed which took up most of the space. It was covered with a gay red and yellow patchwork quilt.

Rebecca wished that she were right in the soft-looking bed. When she moved towards it her eye fell upon a sampler on the wall above the headboard. On it were two ships worked out in a fine blue cross-stitch and the sentence, "He rules the deep."

A gust of wind suddenly shook the window.

"Do not be afraid, Rebecca," the Grandmother said. "You are right above the sea here. All its strange noises can come to you, and its night mists can curl through your window, but you are safely tucked away. On a sunny morning just look out the window and see the silver gulls and blue waves. The world cannot give you a fresher morning."

The Grandmother bowed her way out of the door with many smiles. "Good night, my child. Take good care of the little one. We are so glad that you are here."

Left alone, Rebecca started to make the little room hers and Sarah's own private home. She unpacked her knapsack and placed her three picture books and two photographs of her mother and father carefully on a little table. The wooden doll was put to sleep in the big bed.

She then burrowed into the contents of a large packing case to bring out two nightgowns. She quickly undressed and washed herself and Sarah. When Sarah was tucked into bed the little girl greeted and hugged the wooden doll as though she had not seen it for years. Rebecca climbed into her side of the bed and stretched out comfortably.

Sarah promptly clambered out of the bed.

"Oh Sarah, don't you ever stop going?" Rebecca whispered.

Sarah trotted to the packing case and returned with a hairbrush.

"How stupid of me," Rebecca smiled apologetically. "I forgot to brush out my pigtails." She could hear her mother say, "Fifty strokes for a tired little girl, one hundred for a fatigued young lady."

As she was brushing obediently, her door latch lifted and there stood a thin boy in a blue woolen nightgown.

"Come in," whispered Rebecca. "You'll get a terrible cold out there in the draft."

Caleb entered stealthily. Immediately Sarah tugged the quilt off the bed to wind about him.

"Thanks, Sarah," Caleb said, as he perched at the end of the bed. He looked rather like a patchworked clown with a solemn face. "I just had to come in. It was so dark and lonesome in there." Caleb nodded to his room. "You can hear every wave in the sea."

Rebecca smiled. "Our room is nice and pleasant. I'll see what I can do to make yours more cheerful in the morning. You can have one of my picture books." She paused and continued thoughtfully, "Maybe Grandmother will teach me how to sew a sampler for your wall."

Caleb's face brightened a bit. "She would never be able to sit still for that long. Remember how she made us run through that whole village? She is the quickest lady I ever did see."

Sarah's feet started to paddle briskly up and down the bare floor. She even huffed and puffed in imitation of her grandmother.

"Stop it," the older children giggled. "You'll have Grandfather down upon you."

A sharp rap sounded at the door. Sarah froze like a small statue. Caleb and Rebecca held their breaths, steeling themselves to look into the scowling eyes. How could they possibly explain the noise to their grandfather?

The latch was lifted and a whisper was heard. "It's only me with a little hot cocoa for my children."

Caleb and Rebecca reveled in warm relief as they stared at their grandmother.

"It's hard to settle one's thoughts for sleep in a new place," she explained. "Something sweet and hot might help you. Put the cups on the table when you have finished."

She was gone as quickly as she came.

The children sipped their cocoa gratefully.

"I haven't had such a good drink in ages," said Caleb as he slowly enjoyed the last mouthful. "You know, if we thought of living in this place as a kind of adventure, it might not be half so bad."

"I think this whole day has been sort of an adventure," Rebecca answered slowly.

Caleb lifted Sarah into bed. He smiled at the golden

head already asleep on the pillow. "Your pranks are all finished for one day," he whispered. He blew out the lamp and tiptoed cautiously to his own room.

For a minute Rebecca listened to the waves pounding on the rocks and thought of the great, windy ocean and sky surrounding her. Feeling safe, with Sarah close by, she closed her eyes on her new life.

The Store

THE ORANGE sun rose slowly above the eastern end of the sea, appearing so fresh that it might have just been washed by the sea itself. Its light soon filled the sky, scattering dawn mists and changing the edges of the sea from a leaden gray to a deep blue.

The orange light turned to gold. Some of it fell into the windows of the Deanes' downstairs living room. Caleb, Rebecca, and Sarah welcomed its brightness as they sat about the table finishing their porridge.

Mrs. Deane hustled out of her kitchen, her face aglow with the freshness of this new morning.

"Your grandfather and I have talked it over and have decided that children are happiest when they are kept busy."

Her eyes fell with a soft kindness on each child.

"Every morning the girls will help me in the house. I can teach Rebecca a great deal of things, spinning, sewing, fine stitching and embroidery. Sarah can be my helper."

"Yes," Sarah replied happily, and promptly retreated to the kitchen to bring forth a broom four times the size of herself.

She commenced to sweep vigorously, sending the dust in all directions.

"That's right," encouraged the Grandmother.

Mrs. Deane turned to Caleb, who was staring at his sister's sudden industry.

"Caleb, you are to help your grandfather in his store."

"His store?" Caleb questioned in surprise.

"Yes," Mrs. Deane assured him. "Your grandfather and a man called Jim Peacham own a little store. Jim brings all manner of things out from Portsmouth to sell there and your grandfather, not liking to sail, sticks close by the shop. Now that he's getting on in years, he needs a boy like you to run about for him."

The idea of helping his grandfather day after day filled Caleb with some doubt. However, he was interested in learning that there was such a thing as a store way out here on this distant island.

"What kind of a store is it?" he inquired.

"Oh, it has all sorts of good things to set you to thinking. Fishnets, dried fish, medicines, ginghams, dried apples. It has nice things sometimes, like licorice sticks and cinnamon red-hots. At Christmastime, even toy soldiers and china dolls are on the shelves."

Caleb recalled his father's store at Christmastime, with its rows of bright toys and gingerbread animals.

A sudden banging at the front door and a cold, salty breeze announced Mr. Deane's entrance.

"Ah, there you are," he called, staring at Caleb. "You slept late."

"Yes, sir," Caleb agreed timidly. He looked down at the big boots standing in the doorway.

"A Shoaler must be up with the gulls."

"Now, Thomas," Mrs. Deane came to Caleb's defense, "the boy needed his sleep after his long journey yesterday."

"Well, now that it's done, let's be off with you," the Grandfather continued rudely.

Instantly Caleb put on his heavy sweater and rushed towards the door, half wishing that he could remain in the sunny room with his sisters and his grandmother.

Together, the old man and the boy made their way through the small village of Gosport. On either side of their path were groups of clapboard cottages clustered together, in a haphazard fashion, as though protecting each other from the ocean winds. At the particular corner of the village which overlooked the Star Island harbor was a gray shingled building. It had a good-sized porch and a sign "General Store" in front. The Grandfather stamped his feet heavily on the creaking porch floor before opening the door for Caleb to follow.

To Caleb's surprise, the inside of the store looked like a little piece of his old home. There was the same kind of potbellied stove that had been in his father's larger store. Two sturdy captain's chairs and some plain gray ones formed a circle around it. The walls were lined with the same kind of shelves and counters, but the merchandise was different. There were no fine silks, porcelains, or pieces of jade. Instead there lay a confusion of objects which he had always known, like jack-knives, buckets, jars of ginger, and a score of seaworthy articles. A tub holding a great pile of fishing nets and cork buoys was in one corner. Two barrels, one labeled "Salted Cod," the other "Fish Oil," were on display. In one case were fishing lines and many different-sized hooks. Some were tiny enough to slip into a minnow's mouth, and two were huge, as though worthy to meet up with some shark.

Despite the difference in merchandise between this

store and his father's, there was the same liveliness that comes from a gay jumble of objects. Perhaps in an hour or two Caleb would be able to sort them all out in his mind, but now he was content to gaze at the confused display.

Two corn poppers, several lanterns, some heavy fry pans and wash buckets were strung up on the ceiling along with some dried apples. Many oilskins hung beside the door, and in a nearby case were cartridges, shoe blacking, and corncob pipes.

A thunderous shout interrupted Caleb's inspections. "Hello, Jim, where are you?"

It was amazing that the sound did not send one of the wash buckets flying from its station on the ceiling.

"Right here," replied a low, soothing voice. In the rear door stood a portly gentleman with long, brownish sideburns and a large head of brown curls. He smiled cordially, as though it were his dearest pleasure to be yelled at and to meet the scowling eyes of the Grandfather.

Mr. Deane pointed to Caleb. In a disgusted tone he said, "Here, see what the sea has brought me today."

The fat man strode towards Caleb and put out his hand. "I'm Jim Peacham. Pleased to meet you."

There was a fresh and pleasant light in this man's clear eyes which Caleb could not help noticing.

"Is he a fat porpoise or a mouse, this grandson of mine?" demanded the Grandfather.

Jim Peacham smiled lightly, studying Caleb from head to toe. "Well, the best thing is to call him a man and he'll turn into one all the quicker" was his sensible verdict.

"You're off again, always saying the best about everyone, when the best is further from us than a whale's spray," grumbled Mr. Deane.

He stared at the man and boy as he would gaze at two rancid fish, utterly worthless to him and to his store.

"We'll see if he can at least begin to be a man," he continued glumly, shaking his massive head. "This place is full of morning damp, so Caleb can build us a fire. Go to it, boy. Mind you don't help him, Jim."

The two men stood aside, quietly watching Caleb as he went towards the stove.

Although the Grandfather had succeeded in making Caleb wish that he were a thousand miles away from that stove, a tiny bit of merriment began to awaken within him. Had Mr. Deane asked him to mend a net or split a fish he would have seemed an utter fool, but to build a fire. . . . Had he not spent most of his life building morning fires in his father's shop?

He approached the stove hoping that it would be the

old friend that he thought it was. He shook down the ashes and put in new coals. After crumpling up some newspaper, he placed it on top of the coals. Finally the kindling was carefully arranged.

From close by he heard his father's often-repeated words: "Set the lighter things on top. Then the fire will seep down and keep the coals aglow for a long winter's day."

Carefully he lit a phosphorus match and touched the paper with it. When a flame burst forth he snapped the stove door shut.

The Grandfather blinked uneasily and shuffled his feet. Jim Peacham smiled broadly, like a piece of sunshine dispelling a portion of the morning mist. Speechless, they both stared at the stove for what seemed like hours to Caleb. When the fire could be heard crackling pleasantly the Grandfather stepped forward to put his hand on the stove. He withdrew it quickly and nodded.

Jim Peacham immediately shook Caleb's hand. "Well done, lad," he laughed. His brown curls shook with pleasure.

Mr. Deane gave Caleb a sharp, sidelong glance. He spoke with his customary gruffness. "You might really be of some help around here, boy, but don't let this turn your head. I'm going off to salt and pack some

cod, but you're to sweep down this shop, dust the merchandise, see that the windows shine, and get Jim to
show you how to count money. And when I get back
I want to hear that you've attended to half a dozen
customers."

He drew his breath, turned and stamped out of the
shop, slamming the door behind him.

Caleb looked up at Jim shyly. They both gradually
began to smile.

"It's a rare moment when Mr. Deane closes the door
softly," Jim Peacham confided.

Customers

CALEB set to work doing the chores his grandfather had ordered. His broom sent the dust flying from under the counters. It broke hidden cobwebs, sending spiders scurrying from their accustomed homes.

Jim brought Caleb a bucket of water with which to wash the store's front windows. Caleb attacked the windows, making each pane glisten in the clear morning light. He had to slow down when he reached the top panes, for fear that he might knock the hardware and dried apples from their ceiling ropes. After a while his shoulders began to ache and he became tired of knocking his head against dangling pots and pans.

"Well done, lad." Jim's genial voice came from behind him. " 'Tis a pleasure to see a body so young and hearty put this old store into shipshape order."

Caleb smiled at the compliment. "Do you think he'll like it?" he asked quietly.

"He'd be a fool if he didn't," Jim replied.

The image of the Grandfather's stern face melted away as Jim continued, "And now, lad, you and I have a counting lesson to do."

Jim opened Mr. Deane's strongbox and tossed some coins upon the counter. Caleb's swiftness at figures amazed his teacher. He took tuppence away from sixpence, a sixpence away from a shilling, eight shillings away from a pound. Speedily he added sixpence to eightpence, a pound to a half crown, five shillings to three pounds, and sped through other problems which Jim, himself, had often been in doubt about.

"Why, lad," Jim smiled down at him, "I'm no teacher for you. Seems that you've already been taught."

Caleb nodded solemnly. His father had spent many afternoons doing sums and counting coins with his son. At the time, Caleb had kept wriggling and staring out of the windows, for he longed to be playing mumblety-peg with his friends or out climbing trees.

"If only he could see that his lessons did do me some good after all," Caleb thought sadly.

The shop door opened, interrupting Caleb's reminiscences. He looked up to see the first customer of the morning. She was a lady dressed completely in dark green. Her full skirts rustled, her cape fell in heavy folds behind her, and a green hat, ornamented by a thick ostrich plume, sat heavily on her head. Her face was a severe pattern of hard lines and angles. She walked with her craggy nose pointed high in the air.

"Good morning, Mr. Peacham," she said as she swept by Jim on her way to the needlework counter.

Jim straightened up. Caleb felt that Jim was standing at attention while a captain inspected his ship.

An anxious silence fell while Jim waited for his captain's criticisms. They finally came with a long sigh and a harsh, whining voice.

"No silk thread today."

"No, ma'am."

"But you said that you were going to get it in last week."

"I looked all over Portsmouth but no one had it, ma'am."

"All I asked for was a spool of silk thread. I didn't ask for a golden vase or a silver urn. It seems odd that you couldn't even get thread for me."

Mrs. Brown eyed Jim severely.

"Sorry, ma'am," Jim said apologetically. Seeing that his answer was not enough he continued, "Folks don't seem to need silk thread around here."

"Your customers, if that is what you mean by 'folks,' don't seem to need anything which is at all fine or nice," Mrs. Brown replied, her words framed in freezing ice.

Knowing that Mrs. Brown's tongue was too much for him, Jim remained silent.

An uncomfortable moment of sighs and discontented murmurs passed by. It was concluded by an abrupt question: "May I have the smelling salts I ordered?"

For an instant Jim closed his eyes as though he could not face his next words: "Sorry, ma'am, I couldn't get them either."

This was clearly too much for Mrs. Brown. She rolled her eyes to the ceiling in disgust.

"What is a lady supposed to do, transplanted out here on this deserted island?" she demanded, her sharp voice reaching a higher note. "There are times when I simply cannot stand the sound of another roaring breaker, and the sight of these fish-stained villagers is enough to hurt any lady's eyes. I need my smelling salts. Remember that, Jim Peacham, my smelling salts."

The lady stalked out of the store, leaving Jim Peacham to shrug his shoulders, muttering almost crossly, "I'll remember. I'll remember."

When he faced the bewildered Caleb his easygoing manner began to return.

"Don't worry, lad. She's the one sour apple in our bunch of customers."

"But she was wearing such fine things," Caleb said. "Like she was all set to go to the city."

Jim Peacham laughed. "Ah yes. Mrs. Brown dresses very well for herself way out here. You see, she spent all her life, except for the past seven years, in Salem, and she's not yet gotten used to our Gosport ways."

Caleb listened, interested that there was someone else who came from Salem.

"Your father probably knew her husband. He was a wealthy sea captain, Captain Joseph Brown. The Browns lived in a fine house and Mrs. Brown, if we are to believe her, was the most elegant lady in Salem until one day the captain decided to retire from business. He sold his ship and moved out here.

"The captain once told me that he just wanted to sit and smoke his pipe and enjoy the sound of the sea rather than to be beating about in it all the time trying to make money. Well, you can guess how much Mrs. Brown liked moving out here."

Jim Peacham and Caleb both laughed as they recalled their recent customer, her green ostrich plume trembling with her anger.

"Mrs. Brown came out here with four trunks and her fine things all done up in barrels. Well, most of her barrels are still unpacked. She says that her cottage is too shabby a place for her fine china and linens to be seen in. That's sort of how she feels about the whole island. It's simply not good enough for her, and no one is fine enough for her to be neighborly with. She's kind of sad," Jim concluded thoughtfully.

"But she is so cross," exclaimed Caleb.

"As cross as a dull winter morning. It all comes from her being so twisted up."

A wild scrambling was heard upon the porch.

"Ah, here is what you need, Caleb," Jim called pleasantly. "Here are some customers in high good humor."

The door was flung open and in burst four noisy, barefooted boys, breathless from racing across the rocks. Following close behind was a fifth boy. He had a mop of tangled red hair and snapping eyes which seemed to have the wild sea winds in them.

Caleb instantly recognized the boys as those he had seen on the previous evening playing tag on the small, pebbly beach.

He stepped forward to meet these new customers.

"Hey, I remember you," shouted the redhead. "You were the scaredy cat climbing out of Isaac Mason's dory yesterday. What was wrong? Seasick or something?"

The boy doubled over in mock imitation of Caleb clutching his stomach and groaning.

A shout of laughter came from the other boys. Jim raised his hand to silence them.

"Mind your manners, lads. This is Caleb Deane, Mr. Deane's grandson."

At this pronouncement some of the boys stared at Caleb with open mouths as though wondering, "Who would dare be Mr. Deane's grandson?"

"He is going to help us at the store. He has come to live here in Gosport and it would be a fine thing if you would take him for your friend. Now step up here, Reuben, Joe, and Thomas, and shake hands with the lad."

Jim Peacham flung his arm out in the direction of the three boys. "These are my sons, a right scraggly bunch. Reuben here, he's the oldest and will show you around."

Reuben came forward to shake Caleb's hand. "Pleased to meet you."

Caleb looked into his cheerful blue eyes and at the brown curls which were so like his father's, and instantly knew that he would like him.

"These are my brothers," Reuben stated happily.

"Joe and Thomas." The two boys drew closer and smiled at Caleb in an honest welcome. "The others are our friends, Martin and Tad. Tad's the redhead."

Martin nodded solemnly to Caleb while Tad turned his back abruptly and stared out of the front window.

"Boys, Caleb's grandfather wants him to wait on some customers this morning, so step right up and let him help you," Jim announced.

The boys looked at each other in quick, questioning glances and exchanged several whispers. Reuben finally spoke up.

"But Pa, I'm the only one who has any money in his pocket and that's only threepence."

"Never you mind that." Jim jangled some coins in his breeches' pocket. "I'll give you each tuppence and then Caleb can help you to any confection at that price."

"Hurrah!" the boys shouted, and crowded about Jim.

One by one Caleb hastily filled the boys' hands with cinnamon red-hots, peppermint sticks, and licorice.

Reuben was the last customer. He gave Caleb his money, saying, "After work, you come down to the dock. We'll all go out exploring."

Caleb smiled in anticipation of becoming better acquainted with his new friend.

"Enough is enough!"

The boys wheeled around, knowing full well to whom the deep voice belonged. Instantly they scurried out, their mouths crammed with candy.

"What sort of a hurricane have you brought in here?" Mr. Deane asked, scowling hard at Caleb.

6

The Grandfather's
Closet

A THREATENING hush spread over the store. Caleb
deftly put his change away, trying not to let the coins
clink against the iron box. All the while he felt his
grandfather's light-blue eyes taking in his every ges-
ture.

"Children. Children. Children all over the place.
And then to come in here and find my store overrun
with more urchins," grumbled the old man.

"Oh, the lad did a fine job of waiting on your customers," said Jim calmly, appearing unaware of any
crossness.

"Customers. No customers of mine. They're just
more trouble."

The old man held up a brown-paper parcel.

"See this," he said in disgust. "It's the lad's and my lunch. A while ago I went by the cottage to say that we'd be back for lunch soon. What do you think my wife did?"

Jim shook his head in silence, well realizing that it was best to let the old man get the grumbling out of his system.

"She said, 'Here, take this. It's your lunch,' and shoved this grub at me. The baby girl, the one that's always under your feet, upset our boiling fish, so we have nothing to eat but sandwiches."

" 'Tis a pity," Jim said. "But it could be worse."

He moved two captain's chairs nearer to the stove.

"Here, you two sit yourselves down. Rest awhile and enjoy your meal. I'll be back after lunch."

A sudden agony swept over Caleb. Jim couldn't go away. Whatever was he going to do all alone with his grandfather?

Jim tapped him on the shoulder.

"Go sit down, lad. See you later."

He smiled, and walked briskly out, not even noticing Caleb's distress.

Caleb dumbly did as he was told and sat down on the edge of the captain's chair. The Grandfather pushed some brown bread and pork onto his lap. The two ate together in a heavy silence broken only by their chewing and the fire crackling in the stove.

The Grandfather stretched his legs out so that his feet rested comfortably on the stove.

He had really had a good morning of cleaning and salting fish. The cool weather was perfect for working and held in it a gentleness which hinted at the approaching summer. Also the shop did look shipshape, better than it had in months, though he'd never let on to the boy. Jim Peacham was a fine fellow, good at counting change and gabbing with customers, but he did not do much with the broom, and the cobwebs and jumbled merchandise that that good man did not see was amazing. Yes, it would be fine to have a young set of limbs and a pair of sharp eyes around the store.

He looked at the thin, pale boy who was anxiously picking up some crumbs which had scattered on his trousers.

"Caleb, would you bring me my pipe?" he asked.

The boy sprang out of his chair. Fortunately Caleb had seen the pipe behind the counter, so he was able to return with it quickly.

"Thank you, lad."

The Grandfather soon was drawing on it quite contentedly.

"Tell me, Caleb, did your father teach you manners?" he asked quietly.

"Manners!" exclaimed Caleb, looking up in surprise.

"I mean, to be quiet and to bring an old man his pipe and to watch out for your sisters."

Caleb was pleased, for he instinctively knew, to his astonishment, that Mr. Deane had noticed this in him and had liked it.

"Yes, he did. And my mother, too."

"It was like your father to. When he was a lad he used to run with a pack of urchins on the island, but he was different from them. He was the only one to say his please and thank you's and help his mother on wash day. Those things show that he put others before himself."

"Did he do much fishing and sailing around here?" asked Caleb, eager to know just what his father had done when he was his age.

"Nay, not much. I did my best to keep him from the sea."

The Grandfather bent his white head and spoke softly.

"A lot of good it did me. The sea got him in the end, as though he were nothing but a bit of heavy driftwood."

It seemed to Caleb that the fog from that chill October morning encircled both him and his grandfather. The ocean had been like heavy gray lead when the fishermen had returned without his father. The shock from that sullen morning would be with him forever.

His grandfather was deep in his own thoughts, and Caleb felt the same closeness to him that he had had with his sisters when they so often huddled together, talking of their lost parents.

The Grandfather roused himself and looked at Caleb sadly. "Seeing you're his son, I'll show you something."

Slowly rising, he strode to the back of the shop, where he searched through a stray box. When he found a key he opened a closet door and beckoned to Caleb. Caleb came forward feeling that he was about to see something very special.

In the closet was a fairyland he had never imagined before. On the shelves were an endless variety of model ships, tiny carvings of fishermen and fish, and many other small objects, such as an ivory set of doll's cups and saucers and ocean scenes carved on what seemed to Caleb to be great teeth. Some of the ships had been magically placed in bottles, their masts straight and their sails sturdy in the glass prisons. The larger models of sloops, brigs, and schooners were gaily painted, and inhabited by miniature fishermen intent upon their work, pulling ropes with all their might or casting their nets of thread into the sea.

A large model of a black whaling ship attracted Caleb's eye. Mr. Deane brought it down from its place so that Caleb could inspect it.

"There she is, the good ship *Fortune*."

She had three strong masts complete with sails. A sailor stood on the forecastle shading his eyes from the sun's rays as supposedly he watched over the flat sea for a whale's spout. In the bow was a small figurehead, a painted lady in flowing robes of blue and orange. There were even harpoons and little barrels for whale oil. One sailor was at the wheel, while others were at work scrubbing the deck or tightening the sail ropes.

The most extraordinary details were the six little whaling boats, three on each side, strung up on the vessel and waiting to be lowered into the sea for the chase. Stout oars even rested inside them.

Mr. Deane studied the whaling vessel with as much pleasure as Caleb.

"Yes, there are my little boats just waiting for the fray. A whaleman's life is a good deal of a waiting life. But see," he said, handing a small picture carving to Caleb, "this is the chase, carved on a whale's tooth, no less."

Caleb held the smooth tooth up to the window for

light. Carved upon it in fragile lines, some so thin that they must have been made with the point of a pin instead of a jackknife, was a whaling boat on the very top of a rolling wave. A man was twisting over the bow in an agonizing attempt to harpoon a whale that was only a short distance from the vessel. The whale was bearing down on the rowers and the harpooner, his jaws wide open, eager to devour boat and men.

"Is that what really happens?" asked Caleb, entangled in the adventure.

"Ah yes, if the leviathan is roused enough. This is the hour that makes up for that special kind of waiting which is the whaleman's lot. The boat is lowered and you bend on those oars with all your might while the waves are thudding in your ears. Your shipmates keep up their courage, shouting, 'Sing out and say something, my hearties. . . . Beach me on that black back.' With luck the harpooner locks his iron in the whale's back. Also with luck he gets a grip on the line the harpoon is attached to and turns it around its loggerhead. This keeps the line from running out too fast while the whale plunges ahead. With a tight line you're off on the sleigh ride, skimming over and under waves wherever the beast happens to take you. As the boat bounds along, the headsman takes the harpooner's place to kill the whale with his lance. He aims for the life of the whale, a spot such as the lung or, if possible, right between the eyes or through one eye to the brain."

Mr. Deane paused, his weather-beaten face flushed. His words were slower, but their tone no less important, as the chase neared its end.

"If the whale's dead the crew can easily pull him in on the harpoon line. But you had better make sure he's dead. Many a boat's gone down on the last count. Generally the crew tow him in gradually and slaughter him with more harpoons and then draw away their boat for fear he will lash the waters in his death agony. Finally, when he is really quiet and the sea a hurling bloody bath, they can bring him in close and then tow him back to their whaling ship.

"Some dreaded times the whale sinks under the waves. The crew sings out in relief. They row easy on their oars. Suddenly, like a curse from the sea demons, the whale rises with open jaws squarely under the boat. Boat and whale shoot headlong into the air and the crew jumps. Some into the mouth, some into the sea, and some get mangled between the leviathan's teeth."

Caleb imagined the whale's great jaws snapping out from beneath the waves. "You mean that the whale can come right under you and eat you up?"

The Grandfather smiled.

"Those monsters of the deep can do anything. Caleb, you'd be in his warm belly in no time and probably find good company there."

Mr. Deane took a plain whale's tooth from the shelf. He unscrewed its top and Caleb saw that it was a tiny cup.

"This is what the whalemen's widows catch their tears in. Many's the stormy night when a lone widow uses a cup like this."

"Grandfather," Caleb inquired shyly, his mind full of forlorn sea winds and of ocean treachery, "did you ever kill a whale?"

The Grandfather seemed to speak from a long way off.

"I was pretty close to one many, many years ago. But that's another story, lad."

He screwed the top on the tear cup and placed it carefully on the shelf.

Caleb stared at the treasures in the closet. They were the most exquisite things he had ever seen. He could have spent hours examining each little figure.

"Did my father ever see these things?" he asked.

At the mention of Caleb's father Mr. Deane quickly shut the closet door.

"He did not" was the gruff reply.

"When did you collect all of them?"

"I did not collect them. I made them." The Grandfather locked the door, swung around, and looked hard at Caleb. "Mind you. Don't let on to a living soul you ever saw them."

The magic spell was over. Caleb's fear of Mr. Deane began to return. The stern lines in the old forehead were set. The eyes glared. Caleb gazed at the large, rough hands and could not believe that they had constructed such delicate ships or carved such beautiful pictures.

The Grand View

"IT's TIME for you both to close up shop." Jim Peacham came striding into the shop, bringing some of the fresh breezes with him. "Where's the lad?"

Jim discovered Caleb at the far counter sorting out merchandise. "What's the meaning of this, Mr. Deane?" he called out pleasantly. "To make the lad do such a job on an afternoon like this."

"The more jobs put to him, the quicker he'll be a man," muttered the Grandfather.

"Take him away. I don't want to see either of you until tomorrow morning."

Mr. Deane looked as though he were about to say something cross, but instead he sighed — a sigh which seemed to say that he had put up with enough of

Jim's foolishness for one day. "Come, lad. Out with you," he ordered.

Quickly Caleb grabbed his sweater and with a farewell glance at Jim was ready to follow.

Instead of heading homewards, Mr. Deane climbed slowly up the path which led towards the stone church. It was on a hill overlooking the village and Gosport harbor. From there Caleb saw the whole of the churning ocean surrounding him as far as his eye could see. Only a few rock islands shielded Star from the full strength of the breakers. At first their ledges appeared

to slope gently down to the sea, for time and the waves
had helped to mold and smooth them. On further no-
tice, Caleb saw that a few boulders and island points
were jagged, as though threatening any ocean wave or
sea swell that sought to crack their granite.

Even on this calm afternoon, when the sky spoke of
peace and sun, he saw waves breaking over some of the
fiercer rocks, their white foam shooting up into the
light and then falling in a cloud of white-blue vapor.
He heard a soft roaring all around him from the waves
plunging on the Star Island ledges, cutting themselves

on its jagged edges, pouring themselves into its fissures only to be pulled out and to return again.

Mr. Deane's voice cut into the distant roar.

"I thought you'd better get to know our islands. Our own is called Star on account of its shape. It sprawls out north, south, east and west, something like the arms of a star.

"The two little islands which help to protect the west side of Gosport harbor are Cedar Island and Smuttynose. They are so close to each other that at low tide you might think that you could easily jump from one to the other.

"Directly across the harbor is our largest neighbor, Appledore. Some fishermen do live there and there's a stretch of good meadow for a few sheep to graze on. The most northern island that you see beyond Appledore is Duck, surrounded by all sorts of vicious rocks. It's not so high but it is our fiercest. Indians used to live out there, and when they weren't stealing from the Gosport villagers they'd be fishing for porpoises, which sometimes swim in great droves off Duck Island.

"Duck's had more than its share of wrecks, as have Smuttynose and Appledore. There's a boulder on Appledore we call Dollar Rock. Once long ago a Spanish ship was wrecked on it and spilled quantities of gold coin into its crevices. At first the islanders were afraid to touch the coins, for fear they would have bad luck and more storms. But their greed got the better of their fear and very soon the goldpieces were all snatched up. To this day fishermen often spend an hour or two searching about that rock for a coin which might have been forgotten in that old wreck."

The Grandfather stopped, and strolled around to the other side of the church. He gazed at some sparrows scratching for seed beside some yellow dandelions. Then his eyes returned to the sea.

"There's the most southern island, called White, with our lighthouse. Many has been the sailor who has found new hope from that light. 'Tis a terrible thing to be sailing along in the dark and suddenly be in a nest of rocks that could splinter your craft in a twinkling.

"That small, sprawling rock to the east of us is Lunging Island, also a nasty thing to come up against in a storm. However, it does have a little harbor, so that with a good deal of luck you might be able to land there and at least drag yourself out of the sea. Folks say that the most beautiful seashells in the world have been washed into that harbor."

Caleb stared at the toiling ocean, thinking of its endless chain of storms and all that those storms could wash up from the bottom of the ocean or from the other side of the world — dead whales, white bones, Spanish galleons, old treasure, fine spices from a forsaken trading ship and even, as his grandfather had said, something as tiny as a seashell. He felt alone in the midst of those distant storms and gales. But they soon melted into the brilliant afternoon which lay before him.

He turned to look at the stone meeting house with its wooden tower and cross pointing to the clear sky. It was strange to think that in the middle of this watery region some men had really built this church. It was the mark of the fisherman's hand in the midst of the blue unknown. The church looked so alone upon its ledge, and yet its clear lines and solid stone gave Caleb the feeling that it could withstand the bitterest of winter gales.

A line which his mother had often read came to him: "The sea is his, and he made it: and his hands prepared the dry land."

"Ah, there you two are. I've been looking all over for you."

The small, wiry form of Isaac Mason rapidly approached the Grandfather and the boy.

"Have you been showing the boy some more of his new home?" he asked Mr. Deane.

"Yes. It's about time he saw this sight of stone and water."

"Aye, 'tis a view to set any lad to dreaming."

Isaac turned to the boy. "And what do you think of our meeting house, Caleb?"

"Its cross almost touches the sky," answered Caleb, gazing solemnly up at it.

Isaac smiled in satisfaction.

"That is how it should be. We're very proud of our meeting house, but it's seen a lot of trouble all the same. In the beginning the villagers cared for it. They built it partly from the timber left over from a Spanish galleon wrecked off Smuttynose. But then that fine building burned down and had to be rebuilt. In fact, this meeting house has had to be rebuilt four times because of fires. There have been winters when this ruined building was very forlorn on its high ledge and not a soul seemed to care whether there was a church on it or not. But now we have built us a fine stone building and pray that not a flame will touch it."

The Grandfather had been listening intently to Isaac's narrative. "Yes, this old meeting house has seen a lot of comings and goings," he agreed soberly. "Do you remember that old minister, Isaac?"

"Which one?" asked Isaac.

"The mightiest one of all," responded the Grandfather. There was a rough undertone of amusement in his voice. "He came way before my time and was both sorrowful and angry about the fisherfolk. He got right down to business with them and demanded that they put aside one day each month, besides the Sabbath, to come to meeting and worship the Lord. When the special day arrived the fishermen came and asked him whether they might put off their worshiping and prayer. Due to the recent foulness of the weather they had lost many fishing days and insisted that they must make up for lost time and take to their boats on this fine day.

"The good minister frowned upon his flock and replied, 'If you will go away, I say unto you, catch fish if you can! But as for you that will tarry and worship our Lord this day, I will pray unto him that you may afterwards take fish until you are weary.' "

The Grandfather paused and looked gently at Caleb. "Take the moral of this to heart, lad," he said. "Thirty men went away from the meeting and five stayed to worship with the minister. On that day the thirty men, with all their lines, caught only four fish. The five which had prayed went out the following day and caught five hundred. Thereafter the fishermen were more willing to obey their minister."

The Grandfather stopped. He scowled slightly, but his tale had left a touch of cheer in his eyes.

Isaac smiled. "Such is the power of prayer," he commented.

Then Isaac became thoughtful for a moment, as though he were plotting out what to say next. He spoke carefully, with some dread in his voice.

"I'd like your leave, sir, to teach Caleb how to fish."

Instantly the Grandfather's former friendliness left him. Caleb saw that he behaved the same way he had when he had closed the closet door on all his treasured carvings. He locked himself in and turned into another person, scowling fiercely at Isaac.

"Leave him be," he replied.

Isaac Mason was not to be cast down. "Sir, it is a downright shame for a boy to grow up among fisherfolk and not know anything about their art. I could teach him so easily. I take that redheaded boy, Tad, along with me sometimes and Caleb could join us."

"And do you think, sir," the voice was like low, solemn thunder, "that you have the right to lead my grandson to his watery grave, or that that Tad urchin is suitable company for him — a waif and stray with five layers of dirt on him?"

Isaac's calm eyes stared straight into the Grandfather's. "Sir, I will not try to answer your questions. I only know that the boy ought to have his own head in deciding a few things, so that when he's a man he can stand on his own two feet."

The Grandfather walked a few paces from Isaac and stared out to sea.

Isaac went on. "As for Tad, he's a poor, lone child. Rather than have him fall into bad ways among some of the rough folk here, I've kept my eye on him."

The Grandfather seemed only to hear the distant waves, but suddenly he turned around. "The boy's old enough to make up his own mind about fishing. He alone can sign his own death warrant. The fault won't lie at my door. Only both of you go away. I've had enough trouble with the sea. Leave me be."

They went hastily away from the old man, who had turned his back on them and was gazing over at White Island.

8

The Contest

As the fisherman and the boy walked in silence down to the Gosport pier, Caleb had a heavy sense of gloom. He did not see how he was to encounter Mr. Deane's enraged eyes and storming voice day after day. Perhaps sometime his grandfather would once again reveal his kindliness by telling Caleb a story or showing him his carvings and that kindliness might remain with him instead of vanishing at the story's end. However, Caleb knew that such a hope would probably never be realized.

Isaac put his hand on Caleb's shoulder. "After Mr. Deane's hard words up at the church, do you think you'd like to go out fishing with me?"

Caleb shook his head sadly. "I don't know yet. I'd sort of like to, but there's my grandfather."

"Well, just let me know when you decide," Isaac answered quietly. "The waves around your ears and a mess of fishes thrashing on a line are something I don't want you to miss, lad."

They were interrupted by Reuben, who came running up. "Hey, Caleb, you came at last." A thick lock of hair had tumbled across his forehead. His tanned, freckled face gleamed in the afternoon sun.

"Come and see what we have," he ordered breathlessly, seizing Caleb by the arm.

"Nothing for you to do but go along," Isaac laughed.

The two boys ran across the small, pebbly beach to where the others were huddled in a circle beside some rocks.

Martin held up a box proudly for Caleb to see. Inside it were several whelk shells, large and smooth, tinted with gentle pastel colors. They moved slowly about, bumping into one another.

"Hermit crabs?" he questioned.

Reuben nodded. "Which one do you want?"

"I can have one?" Caleb asked, surprised that any of the boys would want to give up a crab. Finding such pretty ones was no easy job.

"Sure, take your choice," Reuben answered.

Caleb looked at the soft-colored shells again. One

was pure white. Another was as black as ebony, broken by a few dark-brown spirals.

"Isn't it strange how these crabs choose the prettiest houses," he murmured softly.

He picked a lively crab with a shell of pale blue. A golden hue was spread lightly over its color.

"Good," Martin exclaimed. "That crab doesn't belong to anyone."

Reuben looked at Martin severely and then explained. "You see, each of us has a crab and we race them. I have the beautiful white one, but handsome is as handsome does. He goes to sleep in the middle of a race."

"I have this gray one," Martin said. "He's a scrapper. Will fight with anything."

"Oh yeah," Tad interrupted. Coming forward, he thrust his hand under Caleb's nose. In it was a crab with a small, horny black shell. Caleb thought it was the worst-looking one out of the whole collection.

"Don't you forget it. This one wins every race," Tad announced belligerently.

"That's what you think," stated Reuben. "Come on. Let's go."

The boys lined up their crabs. Reuben drew the finishing line in the sand a few feet away from them.

"One . . . two . . . three . . . go!" he shouted.

There was quiet as the boys watched the progress of their respective crabs. All the crabs really started out knowing that they were racing each other. Caleb was pleased to see his scramble ahead, neck and neck with Tad's. Suddenly some of the crabs appeared to lose their senses. Two turned to scramble back to the starting line as fast as their legs could carry them. As Reuben had warned, his lovely white crab stood stock still.

"Come on, you old goat! I'll put firecrackers under you," Reuben shouted, but to no avail. Three crabs remained in the contest, strolling along halfheartedly. Finally the horny black shell shot ahead and was well over the finishing line as Caleb's crab suddenly decided to take a sharp left turn and speed towards the ocean.

"I told you so. He did it again," Tad shouted, jumping up and down on the sand. "The champion of champions."

"Your crab always does," said Martin gloomily. "It's because Tad keeps him cooped up in his black pocket all day. When he does get out he'll race anywhere, just to get away from Tad."

"Take that back."

In a second Tad had leaped across the sand and was twisting Martin's arm. Martin bit his lip and winced from the pain. The tears started to roll down his cheeks but he managed to shout, "Everyone knows you're the worst cheatingest cheat in the whole world."

"Cut this out." Reuben grabbed hold of Tad's thick red hair and hauled him away from Martin. Tad got loose and faced Reuben with clenched fists.

"We'll settle whose crab is the champion once and for all," Reuben said angrily. "One more final race."

"It's all right with me. At last I'll get it through your thick skulls that my crab's the best," Tad bellowed, at first to Reuben and then to the boys in general.

Calming down, he spoke to Reuben. "If my crab wins I'll keep the slingshot I stole from you last week."

Reuben gazed at the scattering crabs for a minute. "All right, if it keeps you from stealing anyone else's slingshot," he decided.

"Oh Reuben, don't be a fool," exclaimed Martin. "His crab will win and you'll have to give him that fine slingshot which it took you two whole days to make."

"I don't know about that," Reuben answered quietly. "Caleb's crab shows plenty of spunk and yours seems to have racing blood in him."

The lines were drawn. The race was on. Reuben's white crab took three steps and again decided to sit down and look beautiful. The rest stepped along briskly until they decided to scatter in all directions except the right one. Only the black horny crab came to his senses. He turned and scrambled to the finishing line.

"He did it. I told you so," came a shrill shriek from Tad. After doing five cartwheels over the sand he raced back to tell Reuben that the slingshot was now lawfully his very own forever and ever.

"You would have kept it anyway. Why all the shouting?" Martin grumbled as the boys glumly picked up their crabs and returned them to the box.

"Ping." Something sharp shot into Caleb's shoulder. He clutched the spot in pain and looked up to see Tad dancing on a rock, like a redheaded sea devil, with his slingshot in hand.

"Sorry I'm such a good shot. That was a real arrowhead I hit you with," Tad shouted gleefully. He sprinted over the rocks and was away in no time.

9

The Pirates

THE BOYS formed a circle around Caleb.

"Did he hurt you bad?" they all asked at once.

Caleb was still stunned by the surprise of the shot. He felt his shoulder to see whether it was bleeding. The arrowhead must have had a blunt point as it had only left a black and blue spot.

"No, I'm all right."

Reuben sighed with relief. "That's good. Tad's jealous of you."

"Yeah, you better look out," interrupted Martin. "The no-good cheat."

"You see, he thinks that Isaac Mason is his only friend, and yesterday when he saw Isaac row you in to the pier he decided to hate you," Reuben explained.

"Then today when he saw both of you walking down here, well, that was just the end."

"But I don't want him to hate me," Caleb answered, both puzzled and worried.

"Don't pay him no mind. He only thinks he hates you. One of these days he'll end up liking you. Just don't let him bother you."

"Let's do something," piped up Thomas, a plump chap with a cheerful smile.

The fun had indeed gone out of the crab racing for Caleb. He still felt the shadow of his grandfather's anger and now, for no reason at all, he had an enemy.

"Off for the dike," Reuben shouted.

Caleb left his thoughts behind in his pursuit of the boys, who dashed over the rocks, Reuben in the lead. They passed his grandfather's store and were through Gosport before Caleb ever realized that they had been running along its main path.

The rocky terrain finally forced Caleb to slow down.

"There's Tad's shack," called Thomas, who was quite winded now and ready to trot along beside Caleb.

The boys were passing by a number of small, weather-beaten shacks. They were crookedly built, some with peaked roofs pointing to the sky at odd angles and others with flat roofs which sagged in the middle. Rusty stovepipes served for chimneys, and thick gray

smoke curled from one or two. There were no tiny
flower gardens or patches of grass as there were in the
village. Only rocks and thorny bushes could be seen.

"This is sort of like a witches' village," Caleb
thought.

He then recalled his grandfather's story of Solomon
White and realized that the old man must have lived
in this vicinity.

"Tad lives out here with his old, drunken father,"
Thomas continued. His round eyes shone with excite-
ment. "Folks say that the old man steals his rum and at
night he whoops and dances like a wild Indian. In the
daytime he stretches out on his dirty floor. It is crawling with beetles and there he is, as stiff as a log, only
they say he snores as loud as the sea. Why, sometimes
the lighthouse keeper hears him way over at White Island and thinks there's a storm coming up."

Caleb visualized Tad's father, an old man, his face
white against the black floor.

"Ever hear of Granny Beade?" Thomas asked with
some pride in his voice. It was not every day that he
had a stranger who would listen to his tales.

Caleb shook his head.

"She's the witch woman who roams about this island
dressed all in black. Her face is all wizened up and
there's not a yellow tooth left in her head."

Caleb instantly recognized the description as fitting the old hag he and Rebecca had seen on their arrival at the Star Island pier.

"See that old hovel up there on the ledge?" Thomas pointed to the smallest, crookedest shack of all, set apart from everything. "Granny Beade lives there all alone with her dead fish. She casts spells and brews medicines that could set you on fire. Folks say that it is she who churns up our worst storms. Why, she could even make one wave wash over this whole island."

Caleb stared at Thomas. His plump cheeks and round eyes suggested a babyhood innocence, and yet he was a storehouse of wild tales. The words could not tumble out of his mouth fast enough.

"She can even snatch ghosts out of the sky. My pa and lots of his friends have seen one of her ghosts. He's a butcher because he cuts the air with a sharp carving knife. He comes in the quiet of evening and just scowls at you with hollow eyes. The wrinkles in his face all light up and glow in the dark. Most folk just run away when they see him, but my pa didn't. He just stared back. And what do you think?"

Caleb gazed in wonder.

"He melted away. That's all. And my pa says it's Granny Beade who sends him avisitin'."

Witches, ogres, and the butcher could easily step out

of the shacks, which were surrounded by rock and ocean. Caleb felt that anything could happen down among these forlorn sea winds.

Thomas and Caleb had walked out onto a great rock ledge at one end of Star Island.

There they saw the Atlantic stretching endlessly to the east. Waves were breaking in front of them on the ancient ledge. Some were purple and some were green, but the nearer ones were all spangled with a raging white foam.

Suddenly, a few feet away, their companions climbed out from the very inside of the ledge. They looked different from the gangling, tanned boys that Caleb had been playing with and they were certainly more unfriendly.

The three boys, Reuben, Martin, and Joe, walked stiffly towards Caleb. They glared at him as though he were a bitter enemy. Caleb recognized each one of them in spite of their different costumes. Joe and Martin wore pea jackets and skullcaps which were made from cotton stockings. Reuben's hat gave Caleb the answer. It was a cardboard replica of a pirate's hat painted in black and gold. His long red coat billowed in the wind while he brandished a wooden cutlass.

All three boys had stained their faces a dark brown. Two wore patches over their eyes. They squinted cruelly at Caleb, baring their teeth as they encircled him.

"Follow us. The initiation is on," commanded Reuben in a mysterious voice.

Caleb followed, not having the slightest idea what an initiation was. Solemnly the troop walked to a wide split in the stone ledge. With some skill you could slip down one of its rock walls and land at the bottom, which was level with the sea. Waves rushed in at one end of the split but were stopped by a rise in the land and a boulder.

The pirates slithered neatly down to the boulder. Caleb desperately kicked his feet in attempting to find some footholds in this strange wall. He kept clutching at mats of slippery seaweed which clung to the rock.

Towards the end of his haphazard descent he slipped and sat down hard on the flat boulder.

"Green Hand, get up," sneered Reuben.

Caleb shot up and briefly took note of his new surroundings. An oil lamp flickered in the dim light beyond the boulder. Beside it was a dark flag painted with a skull and crossbones. He could also see a large sea chest. A good-sized raft leaned against the ledge.

His eyes traveled from one end of the long split, where the waves were washing in, to the other. To his surprise he could again see the ocean at the farther

opening. A great way off, beyond the long alley of
gray, seaweed rock, the waves heaved and roared in the
afternoon light.

"Why, this crack must travel clear across Star Island," he exclaimed, forgetting that he was surrounded
by pirates.

"It's the great Trap Dike that hid women and chil-

dren from the Indians," Thomas explained excitedly.

"Hush you, Hawkins," Reuben ordered.

"Aye, aye, Captain Kidd." Thomas stood stiffly at attention.

Captain Kidd addressed Martin. "Proceed, Bellamy." Bellamy opened the chest and brought out a bread knife which he gave to the captain.

"It's clean," Thomas whispered in Caleb's ear. Reuben washes it in the sea before he uses it."

"Put out your arm, Green Hand," Captain Kidd ordered roughly.

Caleb, with some trepidation, stretched out his arm to this ferocious person.

"I will now cut your arm. With your own blood you must draw a circle on your forehead."

Caleb clenched his fists and gritted his teeth in preparation for the dreadful pain. The gleaming knife slowly came down upon his flesh, but failed to pierce his skin.

"You had better do it yourself," Captain Kidd mumbled breathlessly, and turned his face away.

Trying not to think, Caleb grabbed the knife and quickly cut his arm. When he felt a trickle of blood he dabbed his finger in it and painted a circle on his forehead.

Hurrahs of relief sounded. The pirates quickly burst into a chant while Martin wound a dirty rag around the hero's arm:

"Dead man's bones. Dead man's bones.
Lone and forlorn is he.
We've got his treasure and plenty to measure,
What care we for he?

Dead man's bones. Dead man's bones.
Our life is upon the sea.
Then set up the sail and away we'll trail
To plunder and kill on a spree."

Captain Kidd shouted in his deepest voice, "Green
Hand, we will forget the lowly name of Green Hand.
I now pronounce you Dixie Bull, one of the great pi-
rates who roamed over these islands."

"Hurrah!" sang out the rest of the group.

Caleb beamed, secretly proud that he had borne the
pain which reaped so high an honor. He silently re-
solved to live up to the glory which his new name im-
plied.

"Don't forget the rest of the initiation," Bellamy
said quickly.

Captain Kidd stared haughtily at Bellamy, as though
he were above being reminded of anything. "Dixie
Bull," he proceeded solemnly, "you must now prove
to us that you are fierce. I command that you walk
over jagged stone to the other end of the dike."

Caleb peered down the gray alley to the farther
opening. In comparison with cutting himself, this
journey seemed like nothing. He started off cheerfully,
leaving the pirates to sit in official silence on their
boulder.

Quickly he discovered that he had to pick his way very slowly upon the rocky path. The light was dim. The ground was uneven and covered with rocks and loose stones. Some rocks were well clothed with thick growths of slippery seaweed. Others were jagged, resembling pointed giant teeth. Caleb crept close to the dike's wall for support, now and again stopping to see where his next step would take him.

The low roar of the sea was all around him, making him feel that he was right under the waves. He might have been washed into the dike by their current, along with the bits of driftwood and broken mussel shells under his feet.

A rhythmic sound of deep melancholy traveled down the dike and back again, forever repeating itself. Caleb thought of the women and children, frozen in terror, who had once hid in this spot while the Redskins burned their houses, stole the belongings which they cherished most, and scrambled all over the rocks in search of them. Those women and children, and the wild fury of the moment, had all gone. It was the mighty waves pounding on cracked ledges which remained.

There was a small black cavern in the opposite wall of the dike which Caleb must pass. He noticed this because there seemed to be a white form standing at its opening. He decided that it must be a beautiful white rock, which he would inspect on his return journey.

As he felt his way forward he heard a curious sigh which was not like the wind or the sea. He continued on, trying not to look at the white object. The sigh came again, but this time it was almost like a woman's sob. Caleb turned and started scrambling back, but before he really got anywhere he realized that it would be awful for the pirates to know that he was scared. Thomas would giggle and Captain Kidd would call him Green Hand, but all the same it would be nice to see them again.

Caleb braced himself for what might come, turned and started his difficult way towards the opening.

The sighs turned into sobs. The sobs became violent. Caleb pretended that he was deaf to them. When he was very close to the white thing he saw that it really was not a rock. It was swaying back and forth, crying hysterically.

He must get to the opening. For some reason he felt that he would be safe there. He stumbled past the wailing form not noticing the seaweed beds or how the rocks cut into his ankles. In a final agony the white thing rushed towards Caleb and was upon him.

Caleb fought back fiercely as the thing first tugged his hair and then got an iron grip on his waist in an attempt to pull him down. Caleb tore at the white form. Its whiteness turned out to be a sheet and Caleb caught a half glimpse of tattered breeches and kicking legs under it. He then was toppled face downwards on the ground.

The fall stunned him momentarily, but he soon felt someone sitting — and sitting rather heavily — on his back.

The high cackling voice of a witch was heard. "I've got you now."

Caleb twisted his head around and managed to see that it was no other than Tad perched on his back.

"All's well," Tad shouted, and his call was answered by a loud "Hurrah!" from the pirates at their boulder.

Caleb found himself laughing from pure relief.

"I scared you, didn't I?" Tad inquired, smiling broadly as he got off Caleb.

"I never *was* that scared," Caleb laughed.

"I'm real good at scaring people," Tad said stoutly, his eyes shining. "I'm supposed to be Betty Moody. It was on that spot that she hid with her three young ones when there was an Indian raid. The baby yelled so bad that she had to put her hand over his face so that the Indians would not hear and get them. She smothered him by mistake."

"How terrible!" exclaimed Caleb.

"Maybe the baby's bones are still here," Tad added, grinning like a wicked elf.

Tad held out his hand for Caleb to shake. "Anyway, meet Black Beard. That's me. I buried some treasure in this dike years ago and I've been hunting for it ever since. Some day I'll get my memory back and find it." Black Beard paused to squint his eyes. Crafty and wicked thoughts seemed to be racing through his mind. Both Black Beard and Tad spoke with singular confidence. "Then I'll be the richest man in all the world."

Caleb looked at the determined figure in the gray gloom, believing that some day he really would find the treasure.

A sound of shuffling and labored footsteps announced the approach of the remaining pirates.

"Did you meet up with Betty Moody?" Captain Kidd asked excitedly, his face glowing from the recent adventure.

"I certainly did."

"Good," he answered in relief. "Now you are one of us. Was it just terrible?"

The pirates listened to Caleb's story. He made the white thing out to be a ghost of the most amazing proportions, who could become small and large by turns and surround him with white vapors. Her wails sounded like the great cry from all the dead men of the sea, and her sobs had made his body sway like a tree in a wind storm.

As Caleb heard his own tale he wondered how he had ever dared to pass the white object. Tad sat listening in a state of smiling satisfaction.

Stories

CAPTAIN KIDD, his gold-studded hat cocked to one side, gazed proudly at his pirate crew. They were sitting about in the dike's gloom listening to the waves sweep in and out. This quiet group and the distant purple waves brought many plans to the captain's mind.

"Some summer night, when the moon is full, we'll put our raft out and head for Appledore. We'll dig for treasure there or even find a sack of gold and silver coins around Dollar Rock. We might even set up camp there and fish for our meals."

The pirates smiled and nodded their heads over this plan, each one glad that summer was on its way.

"Or we could set sail for Duck and spear the porpoises out there the way the Indians used to do," Captain Kidd continued. "I'd love to see a whole school in the sunlight, barreling in and out of the water — spouting spray way up to nowhere, their backs gleaming in the sun. I've heard tell that at night they make the most mournful sounds, much worse than Betty Moody."

Martin, in his guise as Pirate Bellamy, spoke up roughly. "We've got to push along with our treasure digging. It's time we found the loot that the real Captain Kidd, Black Beard, and all those fellows buried around these islands."

"But beware of the spade," Tad suddenly cried, leaping up from the rock where he had been sitting.

One ray of setting sun had worked itself down into the gray dike and rested on Tad's red hair. It lighted up his face so that Caleb could see his brown eyes darken and his chin jut firmly out. His thin lips were rather nervous-looking. Although his face was tanned, two blue veins stood out on his narrow forehead, suggesting to Caleb that this boy was not as strong as he would like people to believe. He spoke, not in his usual high-pitched cry, but with a stern intensity, hoping that his audience would believe.

"If you happen to see a spade that you hadn't seen before just sticking in the sand, don't dig with it.

When you take hold of it and dig, you'll fill your bucket with sand. Then you'll stop digging to empty the sand bucket, and when you return, the spade won't be there any more.

"Never will you see that spade again. All your life you will be thinking of the treasure lying under that spade. Every instant of your days you will be tormented by that hidden gold until you are an old, old wreck of a man. You'll come back to that spot again and again, digging and digging and beating your hands upon the sand and rocks. When you are too old to do that you'll sit and dream about the treasure which must be there but which can never be yours. I know; just look at my pa."

Caleb remembered Thomas's story and thought of the man lying in a drunken stupor on his shack floor with black beetles crawling about his head. He felt that all the pirates were thinking of that man as they now watched the slim figure of his son.

Tad slid down from his rock and began to kick some stones aimlessly. He bent over to pick up various mussel and cockle shells and stuffed them into his pocket. As he watched, Caleb felt a wordless sorrow for the lonely boy.

The others were silent, possibly thinking of Tad's mischievousness or making summer plans. The sound of the sea wove a serene haze around their thoughts as it spoke of time and strength and the endless chain of days to come.

Suddenly a harsh hiss came from the sky. It shot into the sea's steady rhythm like a piece of lightning. The boys started up. An old face peered down at them from the top of the ledge. It was jagged, like the rocks, with an enormous crooked nose and a toothless smile. On looking a second longer they saw not only the face but the whole figure against the sky, wrapped in a black cloak.

"Granny Beade," they exclaimed in unison and started scrambling to the other end of the dike as fast as they could.

Tad alone remained.

"Fraidy cats," he screamed shrilly. "Green Hands. Why be scared of an old crone?"

That night when Caleb climbed into his bed he looked about his small, bare room. Somehow it did not seem so empty as it had appeared on the previous evening. The whiteness of his china basin and pitcher glowed gently in the candlelight. On his bureau were a few shells he had collected that afternoon.

A click at his door latch startled him. Rebecca stood at the doorway, her brown hair fluffed about her shoulders from her nightly brushing. Sarah darted forth to pounce on Caleb's bed.

"We had to say good night to you," Rebecca said timidly.

Caleb smiled, glad to see his sisters after his day's outing. "I have been around quite a bit," he explained. "First to the Grandfather's store and then I met lots of boys and, oh, Rebecca, there are so many stories told around these islands."

"I know what you mean," Rebecca eagerly responded. "I've been with Grandmother all day and it seems that everything she owns has a story to it. Her wedding china was brought here on a day when a big gale sprang up and swept all of it to the bottom of the sea. She learned to make samplers from a sweet old lady who one day just hobbled off into the ocean, and hasn't been seen since. There's no end to the strange tales here."

Caleb laughed. "I thought Grandmother rushed about so much that she did not have time for many words."

"Oh yes she does. She even sat still long enough to teach me how to spin. And afterwards Sarah and I went out and discovered a green patch where the most beautiful buttercups and wild morning-glories grow. We'll pick some for you tomorrow."

"That will be nice," Caleb said softly, resting his head on his pillow.

"We'd better go now," Rebecca said, pulling a reluctant Sarah by the arm. "Good night, Caleb."

Caleb dozed off, picturing a walk which the three of them would take. The sea gulls called to one another, circling under the lowest clouds. Sarah laughed at the white foam shooting to the sky as the waves slashed against a sharp boulder.

Preparations

LATE MAY GALES had chased away the remnants of a cold spring, and the warm days of summer finally came. Lavender and pink morning-glories were winding their way up the front of the Deanes' cottage. Close by, some wild geraniums were beginning to bloom.

"They are our summer ornaments, long looked for and long remembered," Mrs. Deane cheerfully explained as both she and Rebecca bent over their needlework in the sunny living room.

Mrs. Deane had taken great pains in getting Rebecca started on a sampler which was to hang in Caleb's room. She had drawn a design of waves and a boat on the rough cotton and had printed the lettering. Both she and Rebecca had chosen the motto after a morning's search through a large, tattered Bible:

"All the rivers run into the sea; yet the sea is not full." Ecclesiastes.

Rebecca felt that Caleb might like the endless meaning in these lines.

The only trouble was that the sentence was very long when you had to do it in small cross-stitch. Her grandmother had taught her small and large cross-stitching and featherstitching, stopping every now and again to indicate how she should hide knots and stray end threads. It was hard, careful work which Rebecca could not do for long stretches of time.

The Grandmother often cheered her up. "Take heart, you'll outstitch me by autumn."

They would then turn to what Rebecca considered more lively work. It was knitting pieces for a patchwork quilt. A grand quilting bee was to take place in two weeks in honor of Mrs. Peacham's daughter, who was to be married in September. All the ladies of Gosport would gather in the church to complete the quilt by contributing their knitted patches and binding them all together for Mary Peacham.

"It will be a fine time," the Grandmother had promised. "A splendid luncheon will be prepared by all of us. Each puts something delicious on the table."

"Will I?" Rebecca asked, wondering what she could possibly make that would be worthy of such a table.

"I'll see that you bake a pretty cake with my fine white flour."

"Me, too," Sarah chimed in.

"You'll bake corn muffins," the Grandmother said firmly, looking into Sarah's smudged face. "But mind you don't stamp around near the oven and make them fall. Then there'll be not a one fit for such a fine party."

As the day of the quilting bee drew nearer, Rebecca could knit almost as fast as her grandmother. Her needles fairly flew over her stitches.

"We are knitting away all our mornings and most of our afternoons," the Grandmother sang out cheerfully. "But it isn't every day that these islands see a pretty new bride."

Often Mrs. Peacham, a stout woman with three chins, would appear at the door to tell of the latest happenings that had befallen "dear Mary, the bride."

"My Jim has just brought over the nicest china for her. It isn't imported or anything fancy, just a plain white earthenware. But 'twill set well with the hard life out here.

"Her bed linen simply must come from Portsmouth in time for me to embroider monograms on it. If it does come — and it just has to — you must tell me the kind of thread and the stitch I should use, Mrs. Deane."

"It will be my pleasure to help you, Mrs. Peacham," answered the Grandmother, delighted that Mrs. Peacham depended on her knowledge in matters of needlework.

Mrs. Deane really looked forward to helping her old friend. Recently she had heard from the village ladies that Mrs. Brown, the captain's wife, had been taking charge of every detail concerned with the quilting party and Mary Peacham's wedding. This, at least, would be one little thing that the elegant Mrs. Brown would not have a hand in.

"It did not seem fair," she pointed out to Rebecca, "for Mrs. Brown to poke her way into the Peachams' wedding preparations when she scarcely knew them and had not been asked to help. After all, she considered that she was too much of a lady to be friendly with anyone on Star Island, yet she minded everybody else's business."

The Grandmother had told Rebecca a good deal about the elegant Mrs. Brown. When she spoke of her, her voice lost its customary cheerfulness and became very crisp and matter-of-fact.

"Ten years ago she came out here with a boatload of

luggage. Such fine frocks must have been in them, but we've never seen a sign of them except for a few ribbons on her Sunday bonnet. They're possibly too good for the likes of us to gaze upon.

"Anyway, I heard tell that she has three chests of lace tablecloths. There are also three barrels of imported china which she has never unpacked, although the china would set nicely in her large cottage. She says that the pieces are so fragile that the wind might blow them away, but what she really thinks is that this is too lowly a place for her fine things."

One morning Rebecca finally laid eyes on the elegant Mrs. Brown. She stopped at the cottage accompanied by her granddaughter, Prunella, when Rebecca and Mrs. Deane were knitting. Mrs. Deane bolted up from her chair as though she had seen a mouse, and hastened towards the door to greet Mrs. Brown.

"I just stepped in to see how your knitting for the quilting bee was progressing and to introduce my granddaughter, Prunella, to your granddaughter," Mrs. Brown announced, carefully pausing to pronounce every syllable precisely.

"Oh yes, yes," answered the Grandmother in a flurry of surprise.

It was the first time Rebecca had ever heard her grandmother speak crossly to Sarah. "Oh Sarah, take that filthy seaweed from my parlor and go wash your face. You are forever messing things up."

She scowled hard at Rebecca, which she had also never done before. Rebecca immediately gathered that this was a signal for her to stand up.

"This is my granddaughter, Rebecca."

Rebecca shook Prunella's cold hand and looked into the stiff, white face. The black eyes stared straight ahead, not noticing Rebecca any more than they would a black ant in the distant corner.

"I must remind you that the patches for the quilt are to be eight inches by eight inches, no more, no less," the elegant Mrs. Brown continued.

"I know all that," the Grandmother replied briskly, rather put out that anyone dared to make a suggestion concerning her needlework.

"You had better check them over to see if they are the proper size."

"That is not necessary," the Grandmother stated firmly.

Mrs. Brown drew her head up haughtily and pursed her lips. "Well, if you are so certain about your work, you had better look over your wardrobes to see if there is clothing for your granddaughters which would be appropriate for the festivities."

The Grandmother's cheeks became very pink. "I am

certain that my girls will be suitable for the occasion."

"As long as you know what is expected of you I will depart. Come along, Prunella."

The girl followed Mrs. Brown out the door like a wooden stick doll.

The Grandmother sighed heavily and settled back comfortably in her wooden armchair. Relief seemed to make her look a trifle plumper and had put a new polish on her apple cheeks.

The needles began to click again as she said, "One would have thought that the Queen of England and no other had been here. Well, Rebecca, how does it feel to have met so fine a person?"

Rebecca remained silent, enjoying her sunny spot in the window seat all the more after the recent interruption.

"Oh, my little Sarah, come here," the Grandmother suddenly cried.

Stepping briskly towards her corner cupboard, she said half to Rebecca and half to herself, "I wonder whether there are any of the peppermints left which Jim Peacham brought me last Easter. Mrs. Brown so set me off that I was horrid to little Sarah."

To her delight she discovered three white ones. They each enjoyed one, savoring it to its last spicy taste.

The Quilting Party

A FIERY SUN had started on its majestic journey to the peak of the sky. Its heat was mixed with stray ocean breezes. Its light encompassed everything, the flat sea, the clapboard cottages, the tiny flowers, and especially the invisible hopes which the Gosport villagers held for this fresh new day.

Rebecca and Sarah stood excitedly at the cottage door entirely prepared for the much anticipated quilting party. They were clad in gay red-checked dresses which the Grandmother had made for the occasion. Each held her own gifts for the luncheon table.

Rebecca was particularly pleased with her present, for it was the first cake she had ever baked which had turned out perfectly. Its pale yellow frosting made it look like a round piece of soft gold and honey.

Sarah kept peeping into her box to see whether her twelve corn cakes were really there.

Baking them had been the most bothersome task that she had ever done. She had mixed one delicious batch but Rebecca had tasted it and said crossly, "Too much salt."

Then the Grandmother peeped into her bowl and half screamed.

"Sarah, you put in all the eggshells!" From that moment on, Sarah had no more fun baking. The Grandmother and Rebecca threw her delicious batter away and made her start from the very beginning again. It would have been all right if they had not bossed her around so much, but they cracked the eggs themselves and made her count the spoonfuls of corn meal which she put into her bowl, and they did not even let her pour the salt in. They were so busy making her muffins that they even forgot to let her stir the batter.

Sarah shook her golden head, recalling her trials.

"Are my girls ready?" Mrs. Deane called, hurrying out of the cottage. "Ah, here they are. Neat as two pins."

She gazed proudly at her two granddaughters in their new dresses.

"Just perfect for a summer day," she remarked happily. "Come along now."

The Gosport path was beginning to be dotted with women, old and young, some with little ones in hand, all strolling towards the church. It was a rare treat for Mrs. Deane to leave her chores and enjoy knowing her friends all over again. She was especially pleased now that she had two granddaughters to show off to them.

"Good day, Mrs. Deane."

The bright greeting came from both Mrs. Peacham and Mary. They looked like duplicate dolls with plump, pink cheeks and billowing brown shirts, only one was a trifle smaller than the other.

"Well, I declare, it's Miss Mary herself. The sun's making you fresh and pretty for your wedding day."

"Thank you," Mary stammered softly. A slight blush came over her friendly face.

Mrs. Peacham turned to Mrs. Deane. "I'm so grateful to your pretty granddaughters and all the other ladies for taking time out to help my Mary along."

" 'Tis a pleasure. 'Tis a pleasure," Mrs. Deane fairly sang.

The ladies paused to catch their breaths when they reached the stone meeting house on the hill. There a long table and some benches had been placed near the entrance.

Two gaunt ladies, Miss Heather and Mrs. Brewster, nervously presided over the arrangements. They smoothed the cotton tablecloth and fussed over the two large bouquets of ferns, scarlet pimpernel, and pink rambler roses.

"Mrs. Deane," called Miss Heather. "I'm so worried lest a wind should come and blow our flowers away. Here we are without so much as a tree to shield us."

Rebecca sympathized with Miss Heather's fears. Anything might happen to the table, with its delicious luncheon, on the very top of this rocky island.

Mrs. Brewster turned her lean, tanned face skywards, looking very much like a female fisherman wise in her knowledge of the sea winds. "Nothing stirring. We'll be safe till mid-afternoon at least."

"We'll take your word for it, Mrs. Brewster," Mrs. Deane said rapidly, urging Sarah to put her corn muffins on the table.

The other ladies followed Sarah's example. Mrs. Peacham set down a fine display of blueberry tarts. She beamed so much that round dimples came into her cheeks. Everyone exclaimed, "And where did you find all the blueberries?"

Mary came forth with a tall mound of clam cakes which caused much laughter. "Those cakes will set well in the stomach of a young husband," the ladies announced.

Mary's rosy cheeks turned scarlet. She laughed shyly. "I didn't have that thought in mind."

Soon the table was covered with tempting dishes of codfish cakes, string beans, corn bread, haddock that was decorated with sprigs of parsley, and a fine piece of smoked ham. Rebecca and Sarah were enthralled by the confections. There were jellied tarts, ginger cookies, spice cookies, and butter cookies, but Rebecca was secretly delighted to see that there was only one cake. It stood in gay splendor among the cookies, its light yellow frosting gleaming in the sun.

"We have enough here to feed us and our men for many a day," Mrs. Peacham exclaimed.

The ladies stood back from the table to admire their handiwork. In the midst of their satisfied silence a thin figure, all bent over, came puffing up to the head of the table.

"Can I help you, Mrs. Brown?" asked Miss Heather, stepping forward.

"Certainly not" was the sharp reply.

Mrs. Brown placed a large soup tureen down with an important thud, straightened herself up and announced, "Lobster stew."

Lobsters were a treasure of the sea which the island ladies rarely tasted. Whenever their husbands trapped them they immediately sold them in Portsmouth for a good price. Truly Mrs. Brown's dish overshadowed all the other delicacies, including the smoked ham.

Pleased with the awe-struck silence which greeted her announcement, Mrs. Brown stood at the head of the table like an elegant bean pole. "Prunella, place your cake among the confections."

Straightway Prunella, dressed in demure gray with some lace at her throat, put her contribution on the table. Rebecca had never seen such a cake. It was enormous.

"Three layers," announced Mrs. Brown.

"Mercy on us," Mrs. Brewster exclaimed. "The girl must have been working for days."

The frosting was a fluffy white. Green sugar vines and red sugar roses twined all along the sides of the cake. Five fat sugar roses, in full bloom, were on the top.

"How did she ever do it?" the ladies inquired.

Rebecca gazed at Prunella in admiration. Prunella looked straight ahead, her ivory-white face untouched by any of the complimentary remarks. There was a settled composure in its lack of expression which seemed to say, "Whatever I do always turns out to be the best."

Rebecca glanced at her own cake, which seemed to be a mere cupcake alongside the jeweled treasure.

"Never you mind, dearie," Mrs. Peacham whispered, as though reading Rebecca's thoughts. "It's the plain law. Mrs. Brown and that which is hers always crowds us out."

"And now to work," Mrs. Brown stated, leading the ladies into the small church.

When Rebecca entered she felt that she had stepped aboard a new kind of ship. She was in a fairly large room with walls of thick beams and white plaster. On each side were long windows set deep into the walls, where the midday light poured through. At first she could only see the endless deep blue sky, but on stepping a little closer to one window she saw the waves and a very little of the island. As on a boat, she was close to only the sky and sea, and beyond their changing lights and ceaseless motion was the divine being who created them.

Upon a platform at the front of the room was a small wooden altar. A wooden cross stood upon it. On either side were stiff bouquets of bulrushes and tall reeds.

"It is here where we pray for our fishermen and all the other folk on this island," Mrs. Peacham murmured.

Rebecca pictured the group of women, with black

capes and hats, drawing near the altar on a stormy winter night. Candlelight fell upon the cross as their sober eyes turned to it. For all they knew, their husbands might be forty miles away or drifting towards the jagged ledges of Duck Island, or perhaps, by some miracle, they were sailing into Gosport harbor at that very minute. The winds circled and howled above the church's pointed roof, telling of ancient wrecks of Spanish galleons and British ships and of the few drenched and frozen sailors who scrambled blindly up the ledges of Appledore and Smuttynose.

The voice of Mrs. Brown broke into Rebecca's thoughts and took her directly back to the all-important task at hand.

"We are not here simply to fritter the time away with our idle chatter."

Mrs. Brown went on to explain that the ladies would bind all their pieces together until they had a section. Then a few ladies would bind the sections together until a patchwork quilt was made.

"But mind the order of your color squares. Green, red, yellow, and no variation."

Rebecca sat beside her grandmother, thankful that she had previously been given a lesson in binding.

At first all the ladies worked diligently under the

sharp eyes of the elegant Mrs. Brown, but like children in school, the perfect sunny day and the pleasure of all being together again got the better of them.

Mrs. Brewster piped up, "Mary, where do you and Saul plan to spend your honeymoon?"

Mary was so overcome with blushes that Mrs. Peacham answered for her. "Saul knows of a fine hotel in Portsmouth where they'll spend three whole days."

" 'Tis a pity," Mrs. Brewster answered. "These young people with grand ideas for wedding trips. Why, no sooner had our wedding bells stopped ringing than Mr. Brewster and I went straight to our little home and got to our chores. Been working ever since." She smiled at Mary.

Mrs. Peacham disagreed quite firmly. "I think it's a fine thing for young people to get away. There's many a cold evening ahead when they'll look back on that trip and be glad."

"Wedding trips," Mrs. Brewster scoffed. " 'Tis a newfangled idea that fine folks have brought from the mainland. Why, Mrs. Deane, you went straight to your chores after your wedding."

"That I did," Mrs. Deane answered brightly. "No tripping about for my old man."

Some ladies laughed softly, knowing well that Mrs.

Deane had spoken the truth. Mr. Deane would be the very last man to do something so giddy.

"As for Captain Brown and myself," Mrs. Brown interrupted, "we went to Boston for our wedding trip. It proved to be a very worthwhile experience."

The ladies listened politely to Mrs. Brown although Boston seemed as far away to them as Japan.

"We visited the museums and fine shops. There were many acquaintances whom we dined with. Some turned out to be our lifelong friends." A note of sadness came into her voice. "Although we don't see them any more way out here."

The idea of Boston, with its parks and wide avenues, was so grand that it put an end to the ladies' discussion. Their skillful fingers bound the sections together quickly and they soon completed the quilt. Mrs. Brown and Mrs. Peacham held the quilt up at opposite ends so that Mary could see her gift. There was a clownish gaiety in the bright patches which would warm any room.

"Oh mercy," Mary stammered, taking in the gay display. "It's too good of you."

"It will last you a lifetime," Miss Heather said, smiling.

One by one the ladies filed by the quilt, touching it to see whether it was thick enough. Some peered closely at the knitting and then stepped along, pleased that they had not spotted any dropped stitches.

Mrs. Deane held up Mrs. Brown's corner so that that fine lady could inspect the work. Everyone sensed that her approval would be official. They were like children who had felt that they really had done quite well on a test but that the final judgment rested on the teacher.

Mrs. Brown felt the quilt. She looked closely at the stitches and the binding. She even took out a ruler and measured one or two patches, thinking that they might be half an inch wider than they should be. Finally she pointed her thin finger at a section of the quilt.

"There. See that!" she demanded in sharp indignation.

The ladies stared to where she was pointing. In their confusion they could see nothing amiss.

"Right there," Mrs. Brown declared shrilly. "Instead of the patches being in the green, red, yellow order as I directed, they are red, yellow, green, and that mistake has been made not once, but twice, in the same section."

Mrs. Brown paused for breath and twirled about. "Who bound this section together?"

She glared at the ladies.

The ladies looked helplessly at one another, each one

feeling that she might have committed this terrible folly without even knowing it.

"I know who did it," said Mrs. Brown, "and if she cannot speak for herself, I will speak for her."

The ladies realized that Mrs. Brown's sharp eyes missed nothing, and if anyone knew who had made the blunder it would be she.

"It was Rebecca. She bound the section that is in the right-hand bottom corner."

All eyes turned to the pigtailed girl standing quietly in her pretty pinafore. For an instant something like a smile flitted over Prunella's face as she stared accusingly at Rebecca.

Tears came to Rebecca's eyes. If only a wave could instantly sweep her far away from this spot. She had not meant to bind the patches together in the wrong color order.

"That's what happens when you give a task to someone who knows nothing," Mrs. Brown explained severely.

The tone of her voice grew condescendingly softer, as though she were addressing a stupid and naughty dog. "Rebecca, I suggest that you apologize to Mary for ruining her quilt. Later on you and Mrs. Deane can rip out your section and rework it correctly."

One corner of the patchwork quilt shook rather violently and began to come down. Mrs. Deane's flushed round face could be seen over it.

"Apologize? Apologize to Mary?" Mrs. Deane cried out in annoyance. "Why, Rebecca has thought of nothing but Mary's happiness for days. Is she to apologize for kindly thoughts? Her disordered patches will only remind Mary that her new friend worked very hard on her patchwork quilt."

With that, Mrs. Deane signaled to Mrs. Peacham and together they folded up the quilt in a twinkling. "And now to lunch," Mrs. Deane announced.

Mrs. Deane's haste ruled the day. Promptly the ladies filed out, leaving Prunella and Mrs. Brown to stare at one another in horrified astonishment.

"Never you mind, Rebecca," said Mary as they stepped into the sunlight. "It's as your grandmother says. I'll only like the quilt all the more because you worked on it."

She put her hand on Rebecca's shoulder. "You must come to see us when we're settled in our cottage."

Tears again came to Rebecca's eyes, but this time they were tears of gratitude for this plump, good-natured friend.

Mrs. Deane gave a little scream. "Oh, dear."

The ladies looked at the table to see what was the

matter. Everything appeared as delicious as it had been two hours ago. Prunella's cake was just as splendid. The blueberry tarts were untouched. The ham was still there. The mound of clam cakes seemed as sturdy as ever.

"Whisht. Get away with you," Mrs. Deane hissed, shaking her skirts.

An "Oh-h-h" of horror came from the ladies.

Sitting proudly on Mrs. Brown's soup tureen was a sea gull. He was happily tossing bits of white lobster meat up in the air and catching them in his beak, from which point they could slither down his gullet. This savory sport made him completely unaware of the excited attention he was receiving.

" 'Tis Siras," Mary said. "Only he would dare sit on Mrs. Brown's tureen."

"Get away with you" came a piercing shriek.

Mrs. Brown's ears were as sharp as her eyes. Hearing that something had gone wrong, she came running out of the church and shook her fist at the sea gull.

Siras cocked his head, quite puzzled by this strange woman who was speaking to him in such an insulting manner. Then, feeling that it was not worth his while to argue with her, he glided gracefully above the table, swooped down to take a large chunk out of one of Prunella's sugar roses, and was off into the blue.

"Well, this has been a fine party! Fine indeed! Come, Prunella, we'll find a bite to eat at home."

Mrs. Brown marched down the hill clutching the stiff Prunella by the shoulder.

Mrs. Deane nodded and beamed.

"Accidents will happen. Make yourselves comfortable, ladies."

First the ladies laughed. Then they ate to their hearts' content. The peaceful sound of the sea mingled with the drowsy buzz of some bees who circled languidly about the cookies and cakes. Sarah managed to eat three of Prunella's pink roses, but a goodly portion of their frosting was smeared over her face.

Rebecca was happy that she could take home some leftover clam cakes and blueberry tarts for Caleb's supper.

13

Witchcraft

ON CLEAR summer days Sarah could always be found at her "secret place." Rebecca had discovered a hollow in some rocks which Sarah had immediately claimed for her own. It was just outside of Gosport, fairly near the rickety shacks. Being halfway down a rocky ledge, it was quite accessible and was protected from the ocean by the remainder of the ledge and two huge boulders.

It was there that Sarah watched the waves rising and falling in the sunlight, their crests like billions of tiny diamonds. On mornings after storms large breakers crashed against the two boulders in front of her. She delighted in the rushing noise and the white foam shooting into the sky. Some of its vapors formed minute rainbows of pink and gold before fading into the air.

She was especially pleased when some of the ocean's spume shot into the little salt water pool which was in the middle of her secret place. She had lined the pool's bottom with her favorite shells and pebbles. The still water somehow deepened the purple of the mussel, brought forth the pure whiteness of the clam shell, and turned Sarah's little brown pebbles into shades of gold and russet.

Caleb had given Sarah a starfish, two hermit crabs, and a fiddler crab for her pool. On this particular morning Sarah clambered down to her hollow and immediately checked up on her sea creatures.

"Here you are. All safe and sound," she said happily.

She took out a wad of paper from her apron pocket and unfolded it. "Here is something nice for you to eat."

Her face lighted up with joy, as though she were going to present some rare peppermints to her friends in the pool. Actually she scattered over the water some dead flies which she had recently killed around the cottage.

She saved her prize, a dead grasshopper, for the fiddler crab. "After all, you have more claws than the others."

Satisfied that the fiddler was scrambling towards the grasshopper, she turned to one of the sheltering ledges of her secret place. "And how are you, my Becka?" she inquired softly.

In a small box, resting under a pink coverlet which Mrs. Deane had embroidered, lay a smiling wooden doll. Even though the painted black eyes and red mouth were a bit faded, Becka's smile was always fresh and cheerful to Sarah's eyes. Caleb and Rebecca would have been stunned by surprise had they seen their little sister tenderly lift Becka from her bed and kiss her on the head.

"Did you sleep well?" Sarah asked. "Please don't worry at night. The waves can't take you away and the hoot owls won't come near you. I'll be down every morning to visit."

She seated Becka on a rock bench and set about preparing tea for her. The teacups were snail shells and the saucers were pearly oyster shells. Sarah dipped a large conch shell into the pool and then slowly filled the teacups.

She tore off a strand of green seaweed from the rocky ledge and busily shaped bits of it into green balls for biscuits, which she placed on her saucers.

She proudly put this meal before Becka and sat down herself to enjoy it.

The two ladies chatted happily about this and that.

"And did you know, Becka, that Caleb goes out fishing every afternoon with Isaac Mason and that Grandfather doesn't even know about it?"

Her face turned quite red from giggling. "He will be so mad when he finds out," she sang gleefully.

A pair of sandpipers almost joined the little party. Sarah remained quite still, wishing for their company as they ran along the ledge. Then they abruptly flitted away.

"Oh, Becka," Sarah scolded, "why did you make so much noise to scare them? Now they'll never come to tea."

"Ha, ha, ha" came a loud cackle from the ledge above.

Instantly Sarah looked up to see an old woman draped in black climbing down the ledge towards her. The hag stood in front of Sarah grinning. Two jagged yellow teeth stuck out of her gums.

"This must be Granny Beade, whom Caleb and Rebecca are always whispering about," thought Sarah.

She looked up into the ancient face that was so like yellow, wrinkled leather.

"Won't you come and have tea with me?" the old woman inquired in her harsh voice. It sounded as though a heavy paper bag crinkled in her throat.

Sarah shook her head. Her eyes were wide from trying to take in the strangeness of this wild creature.

"You must come, little one."

The hag squinted her eyes as she looked out to sea. " 'Tis going to storm. You can't stay here and get a soaking."

Sarah saw the gray and purple clouds mounting across the sky. She got to her feet. "I must go back to Grandmother," she murmured, staring at Granny Beade's black robes.

"No, you shan't," Granny Beade half shrieked.

Summer storms gathered quickly about the Isles of Shoals. Rolling thunder was heard over the beating of the waves.

"I've not had a wee one in my house for such a long time. Come along."

Granny Beade's thin, veined hand clamped itself on Sarah's small wrist. She led her rapidly up the ledge and towards the disheveled shacks, some now swaying in the early storm winds. Sarah tried to break away, but Granny Beade yanked her arm so hard that she stumbled. She was pulled along to a forlorn shack that was set apart from the others.

Lightning flashed close to them as Granny Beade opened the driftwood door and pushed Sarah into a dark room. There were no windows. The room was

boiling hot from steam that carried odors of strong herbs and dead fish.

"Let me light some lamps to have a better look at my wee one," Granny Beade cackled.

She lit two oil lamps. They flickered from the wind which blew through some cracks. Sarah saw a fairly large iron stove in the middle of the room with two steaming caldrons on it. Dried herbs, apples, and Indian corn hung from the ceiling in thick clusters.

"Ah, my little one is looking at my ceiling garden," Granny Beade exclaimed. "You see, it's all true what they say about Granny Beade. She wanders all over these islands collecting herbs for her teas, soups, and medicines. She boils them up for days and days and sometimes thickens her brew with fish heads and the finest bits of seaweed."

A thunderclap split the sky directly overhead. Sarah clapped her hands over her ears and squeezed her eyes shut.

Granny Beade screeched with piercing laughter.

"Oh, the fair-haired wee one is scared. She does not know that it's Granny Beade who brews these storms. A streak of lightning here. A ball of thunder there. 'Tis easy to mix, but I will see that no harm comes to the little one."

Granny Beade took an enormous spoon from the

wall and proceeded to stir her concoctions. "We'll warm ourselves up with a cup of tea. You can have any kind you want. Violet tea, rose tea, juniper tea, and we can spice it up with a little mint and cinnamon. Oh," she said, squinting at Sarah, whose eyes were now wide open, "we must not forget to put in the poppy leaves. And what about my sea biscuits with a bit of strawberry jam?"

Sarah managed to nod her head at the mention of strawberry jam.

"Ha, ha. That's one thing the little girl likes," Granny Beade continued as she stirred.

She spooned out the tea into two cracked clay cups. Then she went to the shelf for some biscuits. A large rat jumped out of the tin container. Sarah screamed at the gray animal who darted past her.

"Oh, tut, tut. That's my hungry Sambo. Don't scream at him, I tell you," scolded Granny Beade.

Granny Beade sat down upon the floor and signaled Sarah to do the same.

Sarah sat down cautiously, looking around all the while for the fat rat.

"Never you mind. Sambo has gone under the stove to warm himself."

Granny Beade sloshed down her boiling tea and promptly refilled her cup.

"Now that you've gone and scared yourself, I'll try to calm you with a story. I'll not tell you about the dead Indians who drift into Star Island on the storm waves. I'll not even whisper about the butcher ghost who comes to the tip end of this rock every evening and angrily brandishes his huge chopping knife in the air."

Granny Beade's black eyes rolled to the ceiling. "Ha, ha. Those are good ones," she laughed.

Quietly she looked at Sarah. "But I will tell you something pretty about fairy rings. Did you know that the little mist rings which you see sometimes on the mainland at dawn were really made by dancing fairies?"

Sarah nodded. She took a sip of her tea and was surprised to find that it was pleasantly sweet, in much the same way that a rose or a violet would be if you happened to taste them.

"The fairy rings on Star Island are different. They are made by tiny mermaid fairies who fly in from the ocean. All night long they dance in a ring to the tune of the waves. The stars sparkle down on their flowing golden hair and their silver fishtails. Each fairy wears a yellow buttercup in her hair."

Sarah smiled a little thinking of the fairy dance. The

hot tea and the steaming room had made her drowsy. Her eyelids began to droop slightly.

"Ah, my wee one's getting sleepy. Lie down by my stove and I'll tell you some more."

Sarah meekly did as she was told.

"It's the poppy leaves that were in your tea," Granny Beade hissed into her ear. "They will put you into a deep sleep and then you will wake up to find out that you have turned into a rat."

"Oh, no," cried Sarah, sitting bolt upright in horror.

Granny Beade's laugh snapped and crackled all about the dimly lighted room.

"You will be a white rat because of your pale hair. What a fine friend you will make for my Sambo. And think," she shook her long finger at Sarah, "you can stay with me forever and ever."

"No," said Sarah. "I can't! I can't!"

Tears raced down her cheeks. She knew that she must get back to her grandmother but she had strength only to cry. Moist waves of warm darkness kept rolling over her. She doubled up on the floor, sobbing quietly as the heavy rain pelted on the little hovel.

At length a loud rapping startled Sarah from her deep slumber. She looked up to see Granny Beade open the door.

"Why, if it's no less than old Mr. Deane coming to visit old Granny Beade," the hag cackled.

"I've come looking for my granddaughter," Mr. Deane stated quickly.

"Well, step in. You've come to the right place."

Mr. Deane took one step into the middle of the room. Although Sarah could see through the open door that the sky had cleared, her grandfather was dressed in his heavy oilskins and rubber boots.

Mr. Deane saw Sarah sitting on the floor. "How could you do this to her?" he shouted. "Hiding her away like this. Scaring her out of mind and body. We've searched the whole island for her. I even thought that the waves had swept her out to sea."

He lowered his voice and glowered at Granny Beade's yellow face. "You wicked, wicked hag."

Granny Beade momentarily straightened her crooked back. "Mr. Deane, don't talk to me like that. Granny Beade knows the way you have cared for this child. 'Get out of my shop, don't bother me,' you shout. And when she runs to you and gives you a bunch of pretty fern and dandelion you snatch it and walk away from her as fast as you can. Granny Beade has strange powers, and so she decided to brew up a storm to teach old Mr. Deane a lesson. She hid this wee one away this bitter afternoon to scare Mr. Deane."

The Grandfather broke in, "Enough of this wicked nonsense."

He swept Sarah into his arms and strode out banging the weather-beaten door behind him.

Sarah found herself crying again as she was carried along the narrow pathway.

"Never mind, little one. You're safe now," the Grandfather spoke softly.

"You mean I'm not going to be a white rat?" Sarah inquired through her tears.

"What stories has that terrible hag been telling you?" the Grandfather asked sharply.

Sarah did not answer.

As they passed the ledge which sheltered Sarah's secret place, Sarah slipped out of her grandfather's arms.

"Would you like to see my secret place?" she asked timidly.

"I would," answered the Grandfather quietly.

The two climbed down the ledge to the little hollow. The Grandfather gazed into the decorated salt water pool, and then his eyes spied Becka, the deserted doll, sitting patiently on her rock.

"Oh dear," Sarah exclaimed, walking over to Becka. "Her teacups and saucers have been all cracked by the storm."

"Would your doll care for a new tea set?" inquired the Grandfather.

"She needs one badly now," Sarah replied, shaking her head mournfully.

"I will see that she will have a pretty one," the Grandfather promised.

14

The Beckoning Ocean

SEVERAL summer weeks had passed since the afternoon when Mr. Deane had told Caleb that he would be signing his own death warrant if ever he went fishing with Isaac Mason. During that time Caleb had almost been lulled into forgetting his grandfather's harsh warning. The ocean, which on clear days became a moving blue pond with a fringe of pure white playing about its edges, had gradually drawn Caleb to it.

At first he merely ventured down to its edge, accompanied by his friends, Joe, Thomas, Reuben, Martin, and Tad. There was a favorite fishing ledge on Star Island where Reuben claimed that some lazy sunfish and perch could often be caught drowsing in the warmer waters nearby.

Tad immediately took his place at the farthermost tip of the ledge, where an unexpected wave could easily slap him into the cold deep. "Fishing without a boat under you is the silliest thing I ever did hear of," he jeered loudly. "But we'll do anything to teach this green hand a lesson."

"Don't pay him no mind," said Reuben. He showed Caleb how to unwind his line and drop it into the sea.

All the boys sat completely still, hunched over their lines. Caleb's shoulders began to feel stiff and the sun burned right through the middle of his back. He wished that all the luck did not go to Tad. Five times the fishing silence had been broken by Tad hailing the catch of another perch. Each one was bigger than the last. The other boys remained sullen and deaf in the face of this information, their eyes riveted upon their own lines.

Caleb's mind began wandering in different directions. He thought of the store and then he thought of Sarah and how she could now make even her grandfather laugh. Suddenly he felt a tug on the end of his line.

"Probably kelpweed," he murmured.

The tugging continued. Something was actually lashing about on his hook.

"Caleb's caught a fish," shouted Reuben.

Tad darted over to watch the proceedings. "Green Hand won't have the strength to haul it in," he taunted.

"Bring her in. Not too slow. Steady. Let the fish play a bit," Reuben instructed calmly.

Caleb worked away, his eyes fixed to the end of his line. He was thinking that he might very well be winding the line in forever when a large, black fish abruptly leaped out of the water.

Tad jumped up and down. "Ha, a catfish. He'll bite you for sure and send you sprawling on the rocks."

"Hush Tad," Reuben shouted, and turned to Caleb. "He's a critter you won't forget. Bring him in on the ledge. I daresn't try to take hold of him, but I'll hold the line, and you get a rock to knock his brains out with. Be quick."

Caleb hastily picked up a rock, but it was difficult to get a proper aim. The black fish jumped and slithered ferociously and gnashed at the air with long white teeth. Caleb's rock landed underneath him.

"Look!" Reuben cried. "See how he bites it!"

Despite the hook in his mouth the creature was biting and fighting the stone as though it were a living sea enemy.

Caleb seized his opportunity and hit him with another rock. After some twitching the fish was still.

"You got him in only two strokes," Tad yelled. His brown eyes flashed excitedly.

The boys circled about the strange catch. He was like a miniature sea monster. His rough skin was a dead black and so thick that, if alive, he would scarcely have felt a shark's bite.

"He's one of our fiercest fish," Tad explained. "As bad as a fox shark. A catfish bit right through Isaac Mason's boot the other day. Why, a catfish would split the blade of a knife in two if given a chance."

Tad knelt down over the black corpse. "See that head. Looks just as much like a cat's as a fish's."

To Caleb the worst thing about the head was the cold, stupid smile on its face, a wide mouth broken at regular intervals by long spiky teeth.

"He's as evil as a crazy man with a belly full of rum," Tad announced. "It's too bad your first fish isn't good for eating, but you did catch a big devil."

Tad smiled at Caleb, and Caleb found himself smiling back. His pleasure came not only from Tad's approval but from the fact that he had actually brought in a fish from that seemingly endless, empty ocean.

Word of Caleb's catfish soon reached Isaac Mason. He promptly invited Caleb to go out fishing with him on Sunday afternoon.

"Your grandfather won't know the difference. He's

always smoking and whittling on his back porch at that time."

Caleb did go and had a glorious afternoon watching Tad and Isaac lay down a trawl line off Duck Island.

The following afternoon Jim Peacham gave Caleb leave to join them in bringing in the line. The Grandfather did not hear this, as he was busily salting cod in the fish house.

During the weekends and on other afternoons Caleb slipped off to sea, hoping that his grandfather had no idea of his whereabouts. He was never certain though, especially on the few evenings when he returned home long after supper. The Grandfather would be telling a story to Sarah and Rebecca or whittling a little doll. He would pause to give Caleb a long look, but he always remained silent.

"After all," Caleb kept telling himself, "Grandfather never told me not to go to sea. I was to make up my own mind about that."

The ocean had opened up an entirely new world to Caleb, continually pulling him out to its mysterious winds, making him want to go beyond its waves and echoes of waves, far out into a watery unknown. This mysterious center had forever beckoned to fishermen like Isaac Mason. It had haunted whaling men and pirates and all the others who did business with the sea.

Despite broken vessels, maimed limbs, and splintered
hopes, it made these men always return to the ocean.

Whenever Isaac sailed out as much as three miles off
Duck Island, Caleb felt that he was approaching the
brink of nowhere. The whole Atlantic lay before him,
and at first glance there was a soft monotony about
the scene. Besides the waves there was the ever-chang-
ing scale of colors and then the silver gray of a jumping porpoise or the snow white of a gull's wing poised
against the sun.

Tad and Caleb baited the hooks of the trawl line
with dead minnows. Isaac laid the line, one end attached to the stern, the other to a floating buoy. If
they had a day of fine weather ahead of them they sat
for a while in the sun letting the waves ride over their
thoughts. Then they dropped their own lines into the
sea, mostly for pleasure, for a single line seemed almost
useless when the trawl was out.

Caleb's cheeks glowed with pride whenever he pulled
in a mackerel or a cod.

"Gems of fish," Isaac stated approvingly.

Tad could not bear the way Caleb clumsily cut up
the fish's mouth when he tried to unhook it.

"He's too pretty to spoil," Tad said and dexterously
dislodged the hook so that its wound scarcely showed.

Sometimes Tad went further than that. After beating the fish's head he cut it and the tail off. The belly was split open with one stroke of his pocket knife. He washed the fish over the boat's side and then set to work at taking out the veins and extra bones.

"There," he said on completing the job, "he's a fit meal for your grumpy grandfather."

Caleb admired Tad's nimble handiwork. Secretly he detested the slimy job of cleaning a fish.

Tad was quick in the ways of fishing. His motions were akin to the darting lights on the ocean's foam. It was Isaac Mason's wisdom and steady hand, however, that Caleb most admired. Isaac easily and gracefully accomplished the heaviest chores, such as pulling up the mainsail or laying the long trawl line, weighted down with its many barbed hooks.

Caleb's favorite moment was when Isaac hauled in the trawl. "We'll see what presents the ocean yields today," Isaac would always say.

Leaning way over the stern, he would pull in the long line bit by bit, stopping to unhook some of the catch. It was usually mackerel and cod interspersed with hake and haddock, but often four or five odd creatures turned up.

A lobster was hauled in, indignant that he had been caught by such a thing as a hook. Wolf and dogfish, who were related to Caleb's catfish, found themselves thrashing about on the schooner's floor. Two breams, small fish with glowing red scales, flipped helplessly about.

Once Isaac's whole arm disappeared over the stern, so hard was he pulling on the trawl. Tad and Caleb tried to help him and the three of them pulled and pulled for several minutes.

"Nothing could be heavier," Tad gasped. "It must be a dead man."

Caleb was too busy to worry over such a prospect.

At length an immense piece of gray-white fat was hauled aboard.

"It's a baby whale, isn't it, Isaac?" inquired Caleb.

Isaac looked at the thing and laughed with satisfaction. "Now and again these odd ones are worth their weight," he said. "This one, she's a nurse fish. We must have hauled in two hundred pounds of her. It's the two barrels of liver inside of her that we want. There's oil in that liver."

The large, shapeless piece of gray blubber lay utterly exhausted upon the boat's floor. A pair of watery blue eyes stared out dumbly from the sides of its blunted head.

Isaac scratched his head and smiled. "She looks like the devil, don't she?" He was well pleased.

15

Storm Clouds

THE SEA was always with Caleb. Before going to sleep at night he pictured the schools of porpoises that he had seen off Duck Island. These huge silvery fish would sometimes frisk in the sea spray, but more often rolled heartily about with the waves, simply enjoying the ocean's deep melody.

In the store he wondered just where Tad and Isaac were fishing that day. Would they take a different route and travel past Londoners Island, or would they go beyond Duck again, perhaps as far as fourteen miles out to sea? Maybe this would be the day that Isaac would harpoon a swordfish.

It was so dull to be left behind to count shillings and pence under the eyes of a cross old man.

One evening Caleb strolled down to the Gosport

pier to meet the returning Tad and Isaac. He was not
the only welcomer. Siras screamed overhead and
alighted on Isaac's shoulder to screech in his ear.
Promptly his screech was silenced by a fine piece of
mackerel placed in his beak.

"Tad and I have been thinking of you," said Isaac
after he had greeted Caleb. "I know how it is with you
and fishing. Mr. Deane's always a worry to you. You're
afraid he might find out about it — "

Caleb's welcoming smile vanished.

"You know he can't be fooled forever. He's too wise
for that. Maybe he already knows about all the times
that you've high-tailed it off with us."

"He's never said anything about it," replied Caleb
in a low voice.

"His silence doesn't mean he's dumb."

Isaac watched Caleb's wistful face for a minute.
"In any case, Tad and I have a fine idea. The cod's
been running beautifully at our fishing grounds off
Duck. We thought we'd catch a batch, dry and salt
it ourselves, and give your grandfather the whole barrel."

"That will be very kind of you," Caleb replied politely, although he was somewhat puzzled. A barrel
of cod brought a good price for Isaac in Portsmouth,
and Isaac needed the money.

"You see, it would be the easy way of telling your grandfather that you've been out fishing with us. He'd see the barrel of cod and know that you weren't just loafing at sea, because you helped with the catch. He's been a storekeeper long enough to know a good piece of merchandise when he sees it. He can either eat the cod or sell it, but it will be worth something to him. Anyway, he'll know that you're doing pretty well and mean business, and maybe it will make him come around to letting you go with us much more."

Caleb nodded doubtfully. "I don't know if he'll ever come around."

"There's nothing like a try," Isaac answered reassuringly.

"You'd better agree," Tad burst in. "We've already set two trawl lines out and tomorrow we go to haul them in. We've done all the work this day, so in the morning you unhook the fish while Isaac and I just sit back and watch."

Caleb smiled at the prospect of a full day at sea. It was to be Saturday and he was certain that Jim Peacham could attend to the customers and cover up for him if Mr. Deane came stamping in.

Saturday's sun rose on an unusually clear day. There was not the speck of a cloud in the sky, and a soft purple color crept over the horizon to mingle with the blue. Aside from the waves slapping against the islands, the ocean was as still as a dark-blue mirror. The mournful cries of distant loons were heard across the waves.

Caleb had just finished his breakfast and was starting out of the door when the Grandfather and Sarah came in from an early morning stroll.

The Grandfather placed his large hand on Caleb's shoulder and scowled down into his face. "I know just where you're headed for and I wash my hands of you" was all that he said. Pushing Caleb out the door, he slammed it behind him.

For a moment Caleb stood numbly in front of the cottage, deeply troubled and undecided. Siras spotted him and swooped down upon him, squawking and scolding with mounting fury.

"Oh, all right, I'll go," Caleb muttered, fearful that the Grandfather might come out to see what the racket was all about.

"My grandfather knows just where I'm going," he blurted out when he met Isaac.

"I kind of thought he would," replied Isaac gently. "Don't let him fret you. He'll be pleased when he gets that fish barrel."

Halfheartedly Caleb helped Tad and Isaac pull up the mainsail and cast off. He could not help thinking

of his grandfather all the while. Even when they sailed
through the still waters around Appledore and headed
for Duck and the open sea, a certain dread rested on
him.

Gradually the wind began to rise and the ocean
became more choppy. A low moan floated with the
winds.

"Do you hear Hog Island crying?" Tad inquired.
"It isn't a good sign."

A pair of loons circled low over Duck Island and
alighted, calling to one another. It was the saddest
sound that Caleb had ever heard and spoke to him of
lost ships, and of men who after battling against the
waters with all their might had finally sunk forever
under the ocean's surface.

One loon stretched his long neck, his head uplifted
to the skies, and shrieked. It was like the shriek of a
woman, high and clear, and tapered off into hopeless
broken notes as though the wind had smashed its tenor
into quivering pieces.

16

A Voice from the Waves

THE SKY was a map of dark purple and gray clouds. They ascended one on top of another, as though they were climbing to the farthermost point in the heavens.

"I'm afraid we're in for a blow," Isaac announced hesitantly. "Tad, we better get to the trawl lines and pull them in quick."

Caleb gazed at the choppy waters almost in disbelief. Such a short while ago the sea had been a glassy pond and now it was alive with troops of waves proudly unfurling their white banners of foam.

"Never mind, Caleb," said Isaac. "A new fisherman has to face up to a storm once in a while. 'Twill do us no harm."

"There's a buoy," yelled Tad, rushing back to the stern. He held the tiller so that Isaac was free to pull in the line.

Isaac and Caleb made their slippery way to the bow. The boat rocked violently beneath them. Isaac began pulling in the line and Caleb, forgetting his clumsiness in the rush, nimbly unhooked the silvery cod, knocked their heads against the sloop's side, and tossed them into a net.

After the lengthy job was completed Isaac nodded

at Caleb and shouted, "See, we were right. The finest cod catch of the season and I couldn't have brought it in without you."

Despite the mounting waves, Caleb smiled proudly at the sight of the handsome pile of fish.

"Now on to the second line," Isaac commanded. Tad steered the boat to a buoy a little farther off.

Caleb wished very much that Isaac could forget all about the second line and head for home.

"See how well I beat against this ocean," Tad shouted. "The sea knows I ain't afeared of it." His eyes flashed in all directions and he laughed at the mounting procession of rolling waves.

The second buoy was reached and Caleb and Isaac quietly went to work pulling in the trawl. In leaning well over the bow Isaac got drenched five times by the huge waves. Caleb mechanically unhooked the fish, trying not to think or be afraid.

His concentration was broken by a sudden anguished yell from Tad. "Isaac's caught! Isaac's caught!"

In the stormy gray light Caleb saw that the trawl had wound itself about Isaac's shoulders and was tugging him out of the boat. He rushed to get a hold on Isaac's legs but he was too late. Isaac was swept over the bow.

Caleb spied an uplifted arm reaching out of a nearby wave. For an awful second it was swept away from the boat and then, just as suddenly, Isaac's whole body was heaved against the bow. By chance Caleb managed to snatch hold of Isaac's arm and began hauling Isaac on board.

Isaac had a bit of the sea's power within him. When he was able to grasp the boat with his other hand he shinnied himself up onto the bow. With a final tug from Caleb he tumbled inside.

For a time he just sat there, breathing heavily, his eyes resting wearily on the high waves which were now tossing foam over the sides of the heaving boat. Caleb knelt down to unwind the heavy trawl from Isaac's shoulders. Some of the hooks had pierced through his drenched jersey into his arms and back. Caleb removed them as carefully as he knew how. The pain did not seem to bother Isaac. He just sat there staring blankly at the angry ocean.

At length a sharp gust of wind aroused him as it blew the sloop perilously over on its starboard side.

"Thank you, Caleb," he said quietly. "We've had a brush with this sea, but it won't set us floundering. Tell Tad to get the bucket and start bailing her out. I'll have to cut the trawl line and be done with it."

Even in the heart of a storm Isaac hated to see some

of his catch go. "Seems a pity to let the sea have what's rightfully ours."

He called to Caleb above the wind, "You take the tiller and start heading for home. I'll be with you in a minute."

Caleb could scarcely breathe. His heart pounded loudly in his chest. He had only been given the tiller once, and that on a clear day.

Tad gladly gave up his post. He had had his fill of the great waves for the time being.

"Good luck, Caleb," he said. "Bring her about slowly, and then run her before the wind till you get past Shad and Mingo Rocks. Then point for the other side of Duck."

Tad rushed for the bucket and started to bail as though ten devils were after him.

Caleb peered out into the storm's gray mist, seeing only row after row of dark waves marching relentlessly towards him. He knew that he would never be able to spot Mingo Rock until he was upon her.

"Coming about," he cried. "Look out for the boom."

Above him the white sail filled with wind, lurched over. The sloop skimmed along at a sharp angle to the boiling sea. All hands grasped the starboard gunwale lest they slide into the frothing waves. It seemed to

Caleb that the sloop had turned into a wild horse galloping off into the gray unknown. He had no control over its giddy speed, which might send them crashing into the dreaded rocks or hurtle them into the midst of the ocean.

"Whatever is keeping Isaac?" he almost cried to himself. "He'd better come quickly or else 'twill be the end of us."

About three hundred feet to his right appeared a great mountain of angry foam.

" 'Tis the breakers crashing against Mingo Rock," Caleb murmured, knowing full well that he must stay away from them.

"Bring her up into the wind," Isaac yelled. "Luff, boy, luff."

Caleb was relieved to hear Isaac's sensible voice over the tearing winds and feel the sloop slow its giddy pace somewhat as it headed into the wind.

On they skimmed into the cold sea vapors and the churning foam. It was the center of all violence and Caleb could hear the cries of shipwrecked sailors and pirates going down to the bottom of the sea with their battered hopes. There was the splitting of proud Spanish galleons and gaudy pirate ships as they were dashed against the rocks or were simply torn apart and swallowed into the sea.

"Bring her about, sharp now," yelled Isaac.

"Coming about," Caleb heard himself shout like a well-seasoned sailor. He held his breath and shuddered as the sloop heaved over and a fresh rush of water swept over its side.

"Heave to!" Isaac shouted to Caleb. "We daresn't let the whole sea in here."

The waves rushed under the bow and the darkening sky seemed to bear down upon Caleb. He became flustered with the noise and, forgetting Isaac's admonition and the fury of the wind, jibed.

There was a sharp crack above the mournful beating of the storm. It sounded like a rifle report. Caleb looked up to see that the mast had split clear down the middle and that the mainsail was falling to the deck.

Isaac rushed to Caleb's side. "I'll take over the tiller," he said, staring soberly at the useless sail that was lying in a heap before him. "A boat without a sail is a forlorn thing, but we can still hope. Do what you can to make things shipshape."

Caleb and Tad quietly fumbled about, trying to straighten out the mess of ripped sail, odd lines, and dead fish. They could not see what they were doing. Their fingers were all thumbs. Their feet kept slipping as the sloop heaved to and fro.

The fierce rhythm of the whitecaps brought a dull sense of uselessness to Caleb. What was the good of a boat without a mast? It was nothing but a tiny bit of driftwood being thrashed hither and yon by the giant waves. It would soon be swallowed up like other unknown sailing vessels that had met their fate in the black swirling deep.

"Dear Lord," Caleb prayed, "give me the courage to face my death."

A calm encircled him in the midst of the breakers. There was a deep solemnity about the ocean's steady moans.

He lifted his head to a new sound. It was like a distant voice, probably the cry of a loon. In a little while he heard it again, only this time it was somewhat closer and there was a certain commanding quality about it. The third time it sounded he actually could distinguish some words, but could not believe that someone was out there in the rough sea.

"Ahoy there!"

Caleb studied the approaching darkness and could barely distinguish a small sloop heading in their direction. For a second he was positive that a ghost ship was coming out of the gloom.

"Isaac Mason! Caleb! Do you hear me?" the voice sounded again.

"Someone's calling out there," Isaac yelled to Caleb.

"Ahoy there! You're in trouble!" The voice was closer to them and was suddenly so familiar to Caleb that he could scarcely believe its sound.

"It's the Grandfather," he declared in astonishment.

"Could be," Tad replied. "He knows his way around these waters. Didn't he used to go out whaling?"

"Where's your sail?" demanded the rough voice from the waves.

"Blown down," Isaac shouted.

"Send Caleb over here with your line and I'll tow you home."

"Caleb, did you hear?" called Isaac from his post in the stern.

"Yes," answered Caleb.

" 'Tis your grandfather in Jim Peacham's sloop. He's coming alongside, so be ready to jump for it with our line."

Caleb struggled over to the bow. Crouching down, he felt a heavy coil among the general confusion of wet objects that lay upon the deck.

"This must be the line," he said to himself.

On standing up he saw that Jim Peacham's sloop was rapidly approaching the starboard side. The wind howled through its full sails while the waves knocked the two boats together.

"Be quick with you, Caleb, lest our ships turn to splinters," shouted the Grandfather.

Caleb rushed numbly to the starboard side, where Jim Peacham's sloop lurched and flapped two yards away from him. In the thick gray light it gave the appearance of an impatient sea bird who, sensing danger, is eager to take flight.

Caleb stood balanced on the rail of Isaac's sloop, convinced that he was about to plunge into the churning sea. Holding his line, he jumped blindly out into the dark gray.

"Well done," cried Mr. Deane and Isaac simultaneously as Caleb came crashing down in the stern of Jim Peacham's sloop.

Caleb had been so cold and frightened that he scarcely felt the impact of his fall.

His grandfather stood beside him at the tiller, clad in his shining black sou'wester. His white beard flared out slightly in the wind.

"Up with you, lad. My old eyes are glad to see you. Do you have the line?"

Caleb nodded.

"Make it fast to that cleat," the Grandfather shouted, as the towline began to pay out and the sail swung over with a loud bang and they began to fall off fast before the wind.

"The boy's done you proud this day," Isaac could just be heard calling from astern.

Night had fallen upon the plunging waves. The uneven but wild wind turned into a heavy, solemn hymn of praise to the endless power of all seas and winds. Its strains seemed to come down from many unseen organs in the sky. As Caleb heard distant breakers pound against the far side of Duck Island, the hymn became steadier and more melancholy, singing of forgotten ships and ancient storms.

He watched intently the black figure of his grandfather and noted the strong arms working the tiller and the stern scowl set upon his forehead as he faced the dangerous ocean path. The path must have been marked on his mind as a boy and he had probably often revisited it in his thoughts, for he steered the small vessel perfectly in the darkness, heading past Smuttynose and rounding Appledore.

The White Island lighthouse sent its yellow beams out into the blackness like a great but distant candle. It was a welcoming sight to Caleb and the Grandfather as they sailed into Gosport harbor.

"I believe we've been spared," the Grandfather said in a loud but calm voice.

Caleb drew nearer so that he might hear the rest of what the old man was saying.

"Now that you've faced your first storm so bravely, I guess that the sea is really in you, Caleb. There's no holding you back from learning to be a fisherman, so my prayers will go with you."

The two sloops were now sheltered from the storm's fury by the islands of Appledore and Star. The winds about them had slackened a bit. The giant waves, now diminished in strength, rolled monotonously into the harbor. They brought a melancholy song with them, as though admitting defeat.

17

The Grandfather's Story

A FIRE blazed cheerfully in the Deanes' fireplace. Its heat and flickering light were the first things the returning voyagers noticed when they stepped into the large room of the cottage.

Mrs. Deane sprang forward to welcome them with anxious and kindly words and many hugs for the boys. Then she stepped back to survey the bedraggled group, assuring herself of its safe return.

"Look at you. You'll get fearful chest colds with coughs lasting a thousand years," she scolded, and promptly whipped into action.

Piles of dry clothes were brought out for them to change into.

Isaac and the Grandfather held mugs of hot rum in their frozen hands. Rebecca proudly gave Caleb and Tad a pot of steaming cocoa.

The Grandfather eased himself into his captain's chair at the side of the fireplace. He sipped his rum slowly and gazed into the fire. His jagged face contained the strength and patience which come from encountering many storms and remaining undefeated. He turned his large white head and smiled when Sarah quietly slipped into his lap.

"I thought that you and Caleb had been drowned," she said.

"No, never," the Grandfather laughed. "I'm too old for the ocean to want and Caleb's too tough for it."

"Granny Beade brewed up that storm. All afternoon she was bending over her pots and pans," Sarah chatted on.

"Sarah, what a terrible idea!" exclaimed Mrs. Deane. "Brush those foolish stories from your head right now."

The Grandfather nodded his head, smiling. "You know," he said slowly, "this little girl might very well be right. It had to take a storm to make an old fellow like me see what a seaworthy lad Caleb is."

Caleb beamed over his cocoa cup.

"Now that we've toughed out this storm, it is time for me to tell a few things to Caleb," the Grandfather continued.

"As a lad I fairly lived on the fishing grounds around the Shoals. When I turned sixteen I was so under the ocean's spell that I took up whaling.

"Those were the summers. We'd voyage fifty to a hundred miles off these isles and wait for her to blow. 'Twas a matchless sight — a white column of foam shooting up into the clear air and then falling silently into the sea.

"We had many a chase and many a fearsome sleigh ride but we always conquered the leviathan."

The Grandfather paused and looked thoughtfully into the fire.

"Then I turned proud. I claimed that Star Island had never seen a better fisherman. There was no one stronger nor cleverer than I, and neither wind nor creature could beat me down.

"Finally my hour came before I ever had a thought of it. I was just out fishing in a sloop eastward with my best friend, Jim Peacham's brother Jack. Suddenly the boat jumped out of the waves. It skittered back and we were on a regular sleigh ride. You see, a whale had somehow gotten its tail wound up in our sloop's line and she was diving ahead at top speed, trying to get free.

"Jack, God bless him, went forward and tried gallantly to cut the line, but the boat tossed so much that he was dumped into the sea and left far behind. I was trying to think of how to save him when the whale turned on me in all her maddened strength. I saw those open jaws before the boat heaved over. By chance I managed to jump clear of that hungry mouth, and was left churning about in those icy waters waiting to go down."

A fearful scowl engraved deep lines across the old man's forehead.

"The next thing I knew was that I was thawing out

in the stern of Leon Henly's sloop. He happened to be beating home and had spied me in those currents.

"Afterwards my long agony began. There was a terrible pain in my back, as if all the mischief heaved up in those giant breakers was crackling and simmering up and down my spine. My back was broken and so, I thought, was my love for the ocean. Jack Peacham's forlorn calls for help kept coming back to me and the whale was forever boiling towards me.

"It was your grandmother who nursed me back to life during that long winter when I did nought but curse the waves around us. But that winter was not all evil, for in the midst of it your grandmother bore me a son."

The Grandfather straightened up in his chair. His voice rose. "It was then that I pledged that the sea would play no more foul tricks on that which was mine."

He looked sternly at his audience and then, as though the silent faces represented a portion of truth which he could not bear, he bowed his head and spoke softly and slowly.

"Such a vow did me no good, for my son was swallowed up by the ocean. Such anger did me no good, for it turned me into a scowling, bitter old man. I remained all twisted up until today. Those waves out there shook me up so much that I sort of had a chance to get untwisted. All the beauty of the sea, at her worst and best, came back to me when I was plowing through this storm. I knew that one man's hatred of her would not make one jot of difference to her vast whims. By the time I had reached Isaac's sloop, all the hatred had left me. If I were beaten down by the sea, well, that would be that. I would go to my watery grave bearing her no malice. And with all hatred gone, it is now my truest wish to have Caleb become as able a fisherman as Isaac Mason is."

He smiled at Isaac. Isaac responded with a low "Thank you, sir."

Sarah wiggled out of his lap to put her doll to sleep in a tiny cradle on the hearth. The Grandfather gazed absently at the little girl.

"You know, Granny Beade does have some sense to her. Her storm really brought Sarah to my heart. Another storm, be it hers or not, brings me to ask the forgiveness of my grandchildren for all my cross ways. I want them to grow up loving and knowing these islands, their birds, their fishes, and their seas. Never mind me if I seem hard on you sometimes. After being cross for so many years, it won't go away in a hurry, but remember, always, that your happiness is my dearest wish."

The old man stopped talking. A hush fell over the group, mingling strangely with the winds outside.

Caleb spoke up, haltingly. "We are beginning to know these islands, but I think we will love you and Grandmother most of all."

The Grandfather smiled at Caleb. "Thank you, Caleb. And now we've had enough for one day. It's time to turn in. Tad, you can bunk in with Caleb tonight. Your poor pa's probably in a stupor and has forgotten all about you."

Tad grinned at the prospect of a warm bed. This night he would not have to grope his way home through the winds and the darkness.

The Grandfather rose and paced up and down beside the fireplace.

"And when this storm is over and the moon is full, I'll take you out fishing in the moonlight. That's the time to really see the ocean. It is a dark gold then and tells of all its ghosts and pirates."

"Can Sarah and I go, too?" asked Rebecca, delighted with the plan.

"Of course you girls must come. You've got to see what sort of fish you'll be cooking for us. Sarah will probably catch herself a rare porcupine fish, all bristling with quills, and trot about pricking us with the nasty needles."

Everyone laughed at the prophecy, knowing it might prove all too true.

The waves continued to beat against Star Island as the children quietly prepared for bed. Their thoughts were full of another night when all would be a black gold and their grandfather would row steadily onward in search of a quiet spot. There they could plunge their lines into the golden waters. The waves would gently rock their boat as they pulled out one silver fish after another from the ocean. Then the Grandfather would pull in the anchor and head for their silent home upon the rock island.